Torn Between Two Lovers

Nekoma McDffrw

09/ 2011

Books by Carl Weber

The Choir Director

Big Girls Do Cry

Up to No Good

Something on the Side

The First Lady

So You Call Yourself a Man

The Preacher's Son

Player Haters

Lookin' for Luv

Married Men

Baby Momma Drama

She Ain't the One (with Mary B. Morrison)

Torn Between Two Lovers

CARL WEBER

KENSINGTON PUBLISHING CORP.
http://www.kensingtonbooks.com

DAFINA BOOKS are published by

Kensington Publishing Corp.
119 West 40th Street
New York, NY 10018

All Kensington titles, imprints and distributed lines are available at special quantity discounts for bulk purchases for sales promotion, premiums, fund-raising, educational or institutional use.

Special book excerpts or customized printings can also be created to fit specific needs. For details, write or phone the office of the Kensington Special Sales Manager: Kensington Publishing Corp., 119 West 40th Street, New York, NY 10018. Attn. Special Sales Department. Phone: 1-800-221-2647.

Dafina and the Dafina logo Reg. U.S. Pat. & TM Off.

ISBN-13: 978-0-7582-5270-8
ISBN-10: 0-7582-5270-6

First Hardcover Printing: September 2010
First Trade Paperback Printing: September 2011
10 9 8 7 6 5 4 3 2 1

Printed in the United States of America

This book is dedicated to Walter, Natalie, Denard, and Martha, the people who keep it together for me at Urban Books and made it possible for me to write two books this year. Thanks, guys. I guess I owe you all a vacation.

Prologue

"Wow! Move over, Oprah!" my good friend Egypt shouted, placing a hand on her hip as she strutted into my bedroom, carrying a beautiful bouquet of white lilies and yellow roses. I stood up from my chair in front of my makeup table, spinning around so my matron of honor could get a good look at my yellow-and-white ensemble. "Damn, you look so good I'm thinking about marrying you myself. I don't even know if you need these flowers."

"You know, Egypt, you say the nicest things in the weirdest way sometimes." We both laughed as she handed me the bouquet. "So, how is it downstairs? Is everyone here?" I hated that they had me locked upstairs until the ceremony. I'm a hands-on person, and this was my party.

"I think so. Mayor Wilder and his wife just showed up. At least we know we have someone to officiate the ceremony. So, my guess is it shouldn't be long now before they come looking for us."

I walked over to my bedroom window, peeking through the curtain so that I could see the crowd forming in my backyard. Everything looked in order: The band was starting to play, and most of the people were seated or were being seated. There was literally a who's who of Richmond's African American elite, and all of them were there to pay homage to Leon and me as we renewed our wedding vows after ten years of marriage. By Monday morning, our pictures would be splashed all over page six of the *Richmond Times Dispatch* and Richmond.com as the weekend's most talked-about event. For the next two weeks, I wouldn't be able to go anywhere without someone being all up in my face.

I frowned at the thought—or rather, at the idea that things weren't as rosy as all of my guests assumed. Leon and I were renewing our vows, but it wasn't too long ago that we had been on the brink of divorce. We had been through some pretty difficult times, and this ceremony was our way of committing to the work it took to repair our marriage. So, no matter how romantic the ceremony seemed on the surface, things were still pretty complicated; but I had made a promise to myself to make a total commitment to our relationship, and that was exactly what I was going to do.

I turned and walked back over to my makeup table. I sat down, placed my bouquet on the table, and mindlessly applied some blush.

"You okay?" Egypt asked. "All of a sudden you look kinda sad."

"I'm all right. Just thinking about life." I put down the blush and picked up my hairbrush. Egypt took it from me and gently turned me toward the makeup table mirror.

"Here, let me do that." She began to brush my hair softly. "Don't think too hard about life, girl. Life's a bitch, and the last thing you want is for that bitch to slap you."

"I think she already has, Egypt. I'm just trying to figure out the best way to lessen the sting of the blow." I'm sure Egypt was curious about my choice of words, but she didn't comment any further. I didn't get along with too many females, but one of the reasons Egypt and I got along was because she knew how to mind her business.

"You ever been in love with anyone other than Rashad?" I asked.

"Who, me?" She stopped brushing my hair, as if the question caught her off guard, or perhaps she was thinking about some past love.

"Yeah, you. You're the only other person in the room," I joked.

"Uh-huh, I was in love once before." She sighed. "Lord knows I loved me some Monster Calhoun."

"Monster Calhoun? You were in love with a man named

Monster Calhoun?" I couldn't help but laugh. I wasn't trying to make her mad, but that shit was funny.

"I sure was. That was during my bad-boy phase, when I dated nothing but thugs. And he was as thuggish as they come."

"I guess you learn something new about somebody every day, 'cause I couldn't begin to picture you with a thug, Ms. I-Don't-Do-South-Side-'Cause-It's-too-Ghetto. So, whatever happened to this Monster Calhoun? How come you ended up with a corporate guy like Rashad and not him?"

"Twenty-five-to-life is what happened," she answered without a trace of humor. "He got twenty-five years in the big house, and I grew the fuck up. If I had left my house ten minutes earlier the day he got arrested, I would have been sitting right next to him with a kilo of coke in the fridge when the DEA busted down his door."

"You lying!" I turned my head to look her directly in the face.

"Do I look like I'm lying?" Her dead-serious expression answered that question for me. "What about you? You ever been in love with anyone other than Leon?"

There was a knock on the door, and then, as if he'd heard his name being mentioned, my husband walked into the room wearing a designer suit and looking like something out of *GQ* magazine. I had to give it to him: My husband was fine. He was tall, well built, and chocolate all over. If marriages were based solely on looks, then there would be no need to ask why I was renewing my vows with this gorgeous man. If only life were that simple.

"Great-goog-a-moog-a. Damn, Big Sexy, you look good as a mo-fo! I feel like throwing your fine ass on the bed and wearing your ass out right in front of your friend."

Sure, he put it on thick, and that wasn't the way to talk in front of my friend, but if there was one thing about Leon I'd always loved, it was that he sure knew how to make me feel good about myself.

"Leon, hush your mouth! I can't believe you just said that in front of Egypt," I scolded, even though I loved hearing his compliments.

"Sorry about that, Egypt, but my wife looks beautiful." He eyed me suggestively. "*Very* beautiful."

"You ain't got to get all G-rated for me," Egypt replied. "I got eyes, and she does look good."

Egypt stepped away, and Leon swaggered over, kissing me so passionately he took my breath away.

"How long you gonna be?" he whispered in my ear. "They're about ready to start the ceremony. And I wanna get you back up here to this room as fast as I can. Girl, you got my shit rock hard." He rubbed himself against me, and all I could think was I was glad I was wearing a panty liner. I know I'm a little old to be thinking like this, but that man sure knew how to get my juices flowing.

"I'm just about ready. Give me about ten minutes and we'll be right down."

"All right, then. I'll see you in a few." He kissed me again, and I watched him walk out the door as horny as a rabbit in heat. He didn't have to worry about throwing me on the bed later, 'cause it was him that might be landing on his back.

"Somebody's excited," Egypt chimed in. "I think your husband's looking forward to some alone time with you."

"I'm rather looking forward to it myself." I fanned myself with my hand.

"Now that's what I'm talking about. I hope me and Rashad are still all over each other after ten years," Egypt added.

"You will be," I said as I turned to her. "Just remember to always respect him, even when he's at his lowest, and don't let nobody in between your marriage."

"I know that's right."

"That shit Jerome pulled last year almost cost me my marriage." I was referring to my ex–best friend. We were no longer speaking, because he did his best to sabotage my marriage.

It's not what you might think, though. He didn't do it because he wanted me for himself. No, definitely not that. Jerome is strictly dickly now. Years ago we had a relationship in college, but that was before he came out of the closet. Then we became best friends—until he took it upon himself to "save me" from my husband.

I'm a go-getter. I own my own successful business and have a level of respect within the community. Leon, on the other hand, has gone through periods of unemployment, during which I was the breadwinner. This didn't do much for his self-esteem, and he took to staying in the house most of the time. Of course, my life didn't slow down, and Leon ended up getting jealous every time I went to a social function without him, or even when I went to have a few drinks after work with Jerome. Things got pretty bad for a while, and there were even a few punches thrown by him—though I have to admit the first punch was usually thrown by me.

Still, I loved Leon and was willing to put up with the fighting because I was convinced that better days were ahead. Jerome thought I was crazy to stay, so he took matters into his own hands. He planted in my house some incriminating evidence that made me believe Leon was having an affair. It was so convincing that Leon and I eventually separated, although he'd sworn up and down that he had never cheated on me.

We were apart for about six months, and during that time I started dating a really great guy named Michael. We were happy together, and I thought I was moving forward with my life, until I learned the truth about what Jerome had done. Leon was innocent, and deep down I still loved him, despite my feelings for Michael; so I made the decision to give my marriage another try. Having to tell Michael that I was going back to my husband really turned my life upside down. It was all Jerome's fault, and to make him pay for it, I fired him from my company and stopped speaking to him.

The stupid thing was, as I sat here ready to renew my vows, I missed that fool. If Jerome and I were still on speaking terms, I would have asked him to walk me down the aisle.

I got up and walked over to the full-length mirror, admiring myself. I absolutely loved the sunny yellow-and-white dress I was wearing. If only I felt as cheerful inside.

"You look beautiful, Loraine."

"Yeah, I do, don't I?" I teased my hair with my hand. "Hey, Egypt, do you think I could get about five minutes to myself? I need to be alone for a little while."

She nodded her head. "Sure. I'll be right outside."

When she left and shut the door behind her, I took a deep breath in an effort to calm my nerves. There was something I had to do before I walked out that door and down those stairs to renew my vows. It was something I should have done a long time ago, before things got out of hand.

I picked up my cell phone and dialed a number I knew by heart.

The phone rang three times before I lost my nerve and hung up. Less than five seconds later, the same number was calling me back. I picked up on the first ring.

"Hello," I said softly.

"Hey there, beautiful. I wasn't expecting you to call. I thought you said you had to attend a wedding with the old ball and chain." He laughed. I'm sure he wouldn't be laughing if he knew the wedding I was attending was my own.

"Michael, I have to tell you something."

"Sure, what's up? Everything okay?"

"I guess that depends on how you look at it."

"What is it?" There was panic in his voice now. "He didn't hit you, did he?" Michael knew all about my past troubles with Leon.

"No, it's not that."

"Then what?"

"Michael . . . I . . . We . . ." I couldn't formulate words; I could barely capture my breath.

"What's wrong? What do you have to tell me?" I was just about to try to tell him again when he blurted out, all excited, "Oh my God, you're not pregnant, are you?"

This time, I had no trouble speaking. "Hell no!" I was old enough to be preparing for menopause, and he was talking about pregnancy. Was he crazy?

"Loraine, what's going on?"

I felt my eyes start to tear up. "Michael, I can't do this anymore." There, I'd done it. I'd broken up with him.

"Do what?" He wasn't going to make this easy.

"Us, Michael. I can't do us anymore."

Yes, this was my dilemma, all put into motion by Jerome's

meddling ass. When I told Michael I was going back to Leon, I wasn't lying—I did go back—but a few months later, I started seeing Michael again. I couldn't help it. I was truly torn between two lovers, because I loved both men—so much so that I couldn't find the strength to break up with Michael until mere minutes before I would walk down the aisle with Leon.

Now there was an eerie silence on the line. Had he hung up on me?

"Michael, are you there?"

"Yeah, I'm here."

"Did you hear what I said?"

"Yeah, I heard you."

"Well, say something."

"What do you want me to say, Loraine?" His voice cracked. Was he crying? "I love you. I'm not gonna give up on us. I'm not going to let you end what we have."

"Michael, you have to. I can't do this anymore. I love my husband."

"Please," he scoffed.

"I do love him."

"Question is, Loraine, do you love me?"

I didn't answer.

"Say it, Loraine. Tell me to my face you don't love me and I'll walk away." I was still silent. "You can't do it, can you?"

"I'm married. I have a husband. You know that."

"You had a husband when we started our affair, but that didn't stop us."

"Don't go there, Michael. You know Leon and I were separated when we first started."

"Sure, the first time, but what about now? You weren't separated when you snuck out the house six months ago and ended up in my bed. You weren't separated the other night when I had you singing my name at the top of your lungs."

I felt a stab of guilt at the reminder of my most recent infidelity. Right in the middle of finalizing plans for today's ceremony, I found an excuse to visit Michael and make love to him. I forced the images of our passion from my mind and resolved to stay strong this time. "Michael, I can't do this."

"You can't do this? I've done everything you've asked of me. I haven't rocked the boat one time. All I want to do is love you. Why are you doing this to me?" His voice let me know how deeply this was wounding him.

"I don't want to do this to you. I'm just trying to do what's best for everyone before things get out of hand."

"That's bull and you know it," he insisted. "Things have been out of hand for a long time, Loraine. Answer my question. Do you love me or not?"

I didn't answer. I just said, "Good-bye, Michael."

Leon

1

I eased back on the soft, butter-cream leather armchair when Roberta walked into the room. For us, it had been the same place, same time for almost a year. I'd been waiting for her; not long, only about five minutes, but long enough to wonder if her damn phone had cut into my time with her again. If so, it wouldn't be the first time. Her phone was constantly ringing whenever we were together. Most of the time she ignored it, but there were a few occasions when she glanced at the caller ID and excused herself. Sure, I knew the calls were work-related, and she wouldn't take them if they weren't important, but damn, this was supposed to be my time, the time we spent together.

If she were anyone else, I would have kicked her to the curb a long time ago, but I was a creature of habit, and her pros so outweighed her cons. Roberta had a way of making me feel good about myself. I don't think I could ever find someone to replace what she'd done for me. I always left with an incredible yearning to see her again.

When we first met, I was such a broken man, but with her help, I was starting to put the pieces of my life back together. I was starting to see myself as a man again.

She sat down across from me, adjusting her body until she was comfortable. I immediately noticed she was wearing a new scent. It was a little lighter than usual, but sexy all the same. She always smelled so good.

"New perfume?" I asked.

"Why, yes, it is." She gave me a smile that lit up the room.

I'm sure she was surprised that I'd noticed. She probably thought that, like most men, I didn't pay attention to the little things. But what she didn't understand was that when we were together, I paid attention to everything, just like her. Oh, I tried to play it cool. What type of man would I be if I didn't? But I left no stone unturned when it came to the time we spent together. It was that important to me.

We'd started this little Monday-and-Thursday-afternoon ritual about a year ago. Back then, you couldn't have paid me a million dollars to think I'd still be seeing her after all this time. She was without question the only woman I'd ever let in my head—other than my wife, Loraine. In fact, I'm sure Loraine would be shocked at how much more Roberta knew about me than she did. Roberta was not just my keeper of secrets; she was slowly taking over Loraine's place as my new best friend.

No matter how wonderful she was, though, I still wasn't quite ready to let the world know I was seeing Roberta. I liked keeping things on the q.t., or on the DL, as they call it nowadays. I was convinced that if anyone found out about us, my life as I knew it would be ruined.

Funny thing is, it all started rather innocently around the time my wife and I were on the verge of divorce. Loraine had kicked my ass out of the house behind some old bullshit she called a lapse in judgment on her part. Oh, she was right. It was a lapse of judgment all right—a lapse of judgment called Jerome, her jealous-ass friend. Thank God Roberta was there for me when no one else was. I was under so much stress at that time that I don't know if I could have made it without her. It seemed that fate just brought us together.

"So, here we are again. I've been giving a lot of thought to our last conversation, Leon. Did you happen to do what I asked you to do?" She was no longer smiling. Her face was serious. She wanted an answer, one I wasn't sure I was prepared to give.

I gazed down at her stilettos. There was no doubt in my mind that they were expensive. As was customary with her, they looked brand-new. There wasn't a scuff mark on them. You can tell a lot about a woman by looking at her shoes, and hers almost screamed how classy she was. But, I wondered, how could such a classy woman talk to me about such lewd things, even if it was for my own good?

"Are you ignoring me?"

"No," I replied, but I'm sure she knew I was.

"So, answer my question. Did you—"

"Did I jack off first? Yes, I jacked off first, all right?" I finished her sentence in my own words. I just didn't want to hear her say it again.

My eyes traveled from her shoes, up a little farther. Her legs were crossed neatly at the knees, showing off her well-built calves. She had an amazing hourglass figure, while her face and hair defied her almost fifty years of age. She reminded me a lot of Angela Bassett.

"Leon, are you embarrassed?"

Was I embarrassed? Of course I was! Here was this beautiful woman sitting across from me, wanting to know if I'd masturbated. What was even more embarrassing was the reason she'd asked the question in the first place. You see, I had a little problem in the bedroom. And, no, it wasn't that I couldn't get it up or that my shit was little. I got it up just fine, and I was packing enough meat for two. My problem was that . . . Well, my . . . my stamina wasn't quite what it should be, and I ejaculated a little faster than I should.

"Leon, there is no reason for you to be embarrassed. We've been through this before. Plenty of men go through premature ejaculation. Masturbating before sex should help with your stamina. You just get too excited. There's nothing wrong with being excited. We just have to find a way to harness that excitement."

After all these months, she still didn't get it. She still had no idea how crushing it was not to be able to satisfy my woman the way she wanted to be satisfied.

"Roberta, I don't think I know how to 'harness my excitement.' "

I looked up at her, our eyes meeting for the first time. I was hoping she would understand, as she always seemed to. This had been the topic of conversation between us for quite some time, but this time she tried to hide a frown. It didn't work. Her disappointment was written all over her face, and it was making me feel even more self-conscious.

"Why are you looking at me like that?" I asked.

"I'm just trying to figure out how serious you are about this. Do you want to stop prematurely ejaculating? Do you want to enjoy a normal sex life?"

What was that supposed to mean? Was she taking a potshot at my manhood? If she was trying to humiliate me, she was doing a good job. My embarrassment turned into defensive anger.

I stood up. "Of course I wanna have a got-damn normal sex life. Why do you think I've been paying your sorry ass a hundred dollars an hour for the past twelve months?" I pointed my finger in her face. "I should be asking your ass when I'm going to have a normal sex life. You're the damn therapist—oh, excuse me, psychiatrist! So, what's up, Doc? When am I going to be cured? When am I going to be able to fuck like I used to?"

Roberta sat up in her chair, her bottom lip quivering just a bit. There was no doubt in my mind she did not appreciate my sudden use of profanity or my accusatory tone, but this wasn't the first time I'd gotten loud. Truth is, I just wanted her to snap back at me, give me a reason to walk out that door and feel sorry for myself, but she never did. No matter how ignorant I got, she always kept it professional.

Surprisingly, her face softened. "You know what, Leon? You're right. I'm sorry. I know you're trying. And to be totally honest, I can't say when you're going to be cured. But I'm committed to finding a solution to your problems. I just need your help."

Well, if you haven't figured it out, Roberta is my shrink.

"What can I do?" I asked.

"Why don't you have a seat so we can talk about that?" I did what I was told and sat back down.

"So, I take it you and Loraine made love this weekend, and things didn't quite work out as you planned?"

"I did exactly what you said." I sighed. "I took her out to a nice romantic dinner at Luigi's. When we got home, I went in the bathroom, locked the door, and took care of business."

"Okay, that's good. What'd you do next?"

"I broke out the massage oil and gave Loraine a massage from head to toe. You would have been proud of me, Doc. I took things nice and slow, just like we talked about." My eyes panned her office, which was trimmed in cherrywood molding that matched her Queen Anne desk.

"I'm already proud of you, Leon." She patted my knee like I was a schoolboy who needed approval. I have to admit I did appreciate her words. "What happened after that? How were things afterward? Did you get intimate?" She was trying to get back in my head. She knew we'd gotten intimate.

I twiddled my fingers and wiped my sweaty palms on my jeans, stalling for time. I really didn't want to answer her, because I knew what she would ask next. I finally admitted, "Yeah, we did."

"So, how was it?"

I lowered my head and closed my eyes. Once again, I could see Loraine's look of disgust when I collapsed on top of her within a minute. I just knew that was going to be the time I held out until Loraine reached her climax, but once again, I came too quickly. Loraine didn't say anything, but I could tell she was getting sick of my Speedy Gonzales performances. I felt about as low as a man could get.

"Leon, how was it?"

"Horrible. Worse than ever."

"What do you mean?"

"I tried to hold back, Doc. I tried every trick in the book. I bit my lip, I tried to count, I even tried to imagine her wearing clown makeup, but it seems like the more I try to hold back, the more excited I get. Once I got inside her, that was all she wrote. I exploded like a short fuse on a firecracker—quick, fast, in a hurry."

"I see. . . . Maybe we're going about this wrong. Maybe we

should be looking at the cause of your excitement, not the effect." Roberta gave me a compassionate look, which encouraged me to open up. "What about Loraine gets you all worked up?"

I let out a low whistle. "Wow, I mean, where do I start? She's just so . . . so sexy to me, Doc. I've told you this before. I just love a big, thick woman, and when Loraine takes off her clothes, all the blood in my body rushes right to my groin. She just makes me feel like exploding." I glanced down at my pants. "I'm all excited just thinking about her being naked."

"Yes, I can see that." Roberta averted her eyes. "Have you ever been attracted to smaller-framed women?"

"Not really. I mean, I've been with a few, and I can appreciate the beauty others see in small women, but they do absolutely nothing for me."

"Hmm, interesting. So, when did your attraction for big women begin?"

I shrugged. "I don't know. I've always loved big women. Back in the day, I used to always tell my friends, 'you can have anyone who looks like Whitney Houston, but stay the hell away from anyone bigger than Jackée, 'cause she mine'!"

"I see. Any large women in your family?"

"My aunt was a big, beautiful woman." I smiled at the thought of Aunt Barbara.

"Is this the aunt who raised you, the one married to your abusive uncle?"

"Mmm-hmm, Aunt Barbara was the best. Sweetest woman in the world."

"Really. You don't talk about her much. Why is that?" She began to write.

"I don't know." I heaved a deep sigh before I continued. I was treading in some dangerous waters that I preferred to keep locked away inside my heart. "Probably because like every other woman in my childhood, she ended up leaving me alone. She died when I was in high school. She didn't even get to see me graduate."

"I'm sorry to hear that."

"Yeah, kinda painful, you know."

"I can imagine." She started writing again. I hated when she did that, because it always made me feel like I was some type of case study for some book she was writing. "Was your mother a big woman?"

"Well, my mother passed away when I was five. I barely remember her, but from the pictures I've seen, no, she was about average size."

"How about your father?"

"I never knew my father."

"I see. So, did you and your aunt have a good relationship?"

"Yeah, Aunt Barbara was the best. She was like a mother to me."

"Interesting. Tell me more."

"I can't. Like I said before, she died when I was young. I can barely remember what happened last week. Don't ask me about my childhood."

"Okay, so tell me what you remember."

"Funny thing is, I can't even remember anything about her other than she was good to me, made me feel safe. Every time I think about a woman adoring me, I always think about my aunt." I watched as her pen flew across the page. She sure was taking lots of notes about my aunt. Something about what I'd said must have really intrigued her. "So, is that why I like big women? Because of my aunt?"

She flipped the page on her notebook and finished a few more notes before she replied. "That makes sense. A lot of our adult life is based on our childhood. We are often attracted to people who remind us of our parental figures. It's not unusual for men to look for mother figures, especially with all the physical abuse you took from your uncle. Perhaps your aunt was the only one protecting you from your uncle."

I nodded. "Maybe so. But I don't see what this has to do with me not satisfying my wife."

"Does Loraine remind you of your aunt?"

I paused. "Yes. No. I don't know. Maybe. They both have the same body type."

I was feeling confused. It wasn't like I didn't understand her questions, but more like my emotions were too mixed up for me to make sense of them. Usually my conversations with Roberta were pretty black and white: How did I feel about my uncle's abuse? Bitter. How did I feel about Loraine leaving me? Hurt. And how did I feel about her friend Jerome setting me up? Pissed me off. But now that she was digging for answers about my aunt, I suddenly couldn't pinpoint my emotions.

"What do you think about your aunt that has to do with your issues?"

"Why should she have anything to do with what's going on with Loraine and me?" I noticed my heart started racing. What the hell was wrong with me?

"Let me rephrase this. What do you remember about your aunt that was so kind when you were a teenager?"

I shook my head. "I can't remember."

"Leon, do you realize that every time we try to go back into your teenage years, you draw a blank?"

I hadn't given it much thought until then, but she was right. Everything from high school and earlier was vague. "I do now."

"I know you decided against it when we started looking into your uncle, but I think it may be time we revisited the idea of hypnotism."

The last time she hypnotized me was about three months ago. That's when I found out that my beloved uncle Charles had physically abused me when I was a young boy. My memories from that session were so intense that Roberta had to snap me out of my hypnotic state right in the middle of my uncle beating me with a razor strap. Afterward, she told me I was screaming so loud that she was afraid I was going to have some type of psychotic breakdown. I don't know how true that was, but the pain was so real I could still feel that strap slamming against me, ripping my flesh, to this day. I'd been having nightmares about it ever since and was terrified of the idea of being hypnotized again because of it.

I glanced at Roberta's face. She looked sympathetic, despite the fact that I knew she was pushing for me to go back under hypnosis. "Doc, if it's going to help me save my marriage, I'll do whatever it takes. I'm desperate."

Jerome

2

I was awakened by the cool night air as it hit my naked backside. I was sure he'd pulled the comforter off me accidentally while getting out the bed, so I wasn't upset. I opened my eyes and saw him sitting on the edge of the bed with his pants in hand, about to get dressed. He smiled, reaching over to cover my nakedness. He was kind in that way. Knowing him, he was probably beating himself up inside for waking me in the first place. I blew him a kiss.

The way he glanced at me made everything below my waist start to stir. I reached for him, hoping to get some more of what he'd given me earlier in the evening. Unfortunately, he gently pushed me back, shaking his head to let me know that wasn't going to happen.

I glanced at the clock on my nightstand and then turned toward him with a pout. I felt like I was being punished. What had I done to deserve this treatment? Had I not satisfied him? He never left this early, not on a Saturday night.

I was pissed and didn't bother hiding it in my tone. "You leaving already? It's only one o'clock."

I immediately dropped the attitude and became quiet when he snapped his head in my direction. The angry look he gave me told me everything I needed to know. I'd broken one of his unspoken rules: Thou shall not question Big Poppa when he's ready to leave. I was getting a little sick of his fucking rules, and I wanted to express that, but we'd just had a really nice dinner, watched a great DVD, and had two hours of mind-blowing sex, all of which I wanted to do again sometime soon, so I was not about to raise hell. Especially since this was an argument I couldn't win no matter what I said or did. We'd been down this road many times, and each and every time, I was the one on the losing end, begging for forgiveness. He was going home to his wife, quite possibly to have sex with her after he'd had sex with me, and all I could do was sit there with my feelings hurt, watching his sexy ass get dressed.

"How about a blow job for the road?" I asked in the sweetest of tones. If he would just let me put my lips around his dick, it would be a wrap. I guess he knew it, too, because he flat out rejected me.

"Jerome, don't start."

Don't start? He was walking out of my very warm bed to be with a woman who didn't give a damn about anything but appearances, and he told me not to start? His ass hadn't been saying that shit when he was praising my name as I sucked his dick two hours ago. Anyhow, like I said before, I was getting sick of his shit. He didn't know it yet, but he was going to have to make a decision. My life had been one roller coaster after another the past year, and I needed some stability, with him or without him. I'd put in too much time and effort for him to keep treating me any old way.

You see, what Big Poppa and I had was like Ray Parker Jr.'s song, "The Other Woman," except, obviously, Big Poppa was in love with "the other man." At least I thought he loved me, until moments like this when he got up to leave with no regard for my feelings. Something was going to have to change.

An hour after Big Poppa left, I was lying in the bed watching *Criminal Minds* reruns on A&E. I was pissed off about his leaving, no question about it, but then again, I was always pissed when Big Poppa left. However, I had a plan to improve my mood. I was a believer in that old cliché that the best way to get over a lover is to get under another one. I guess it was a good thing I had plenty of other lovers. There were none I cared about as much as Big Poppa, but what I lost in quality, I damn sure made up for in quantity. Sure, it was late and last minute, but I had men begging to get some of this. Surely one of them would be willing to leave his wife or girlfriend for some fun under the covers with the man who gave the best blow jobs in Richmond.

I reached over to my nightstand, picked up my iPhone, and scrolled through the address book, clicking on the file aptly marked "Little Black Book." I smiled as the list of names appeared on the screen. There were more than a hundred men's names in it, most of whom I'd slept with at one time or another over the past twenty-five years. Some were famous; others were just conquests; many of them were financial sponsors; the majority of them were married. I had this thing for married men or men on the down low, as it was now called, partly because they were a challenge, but mainly because they usually didn't act feminine. Don't get me wrong. I didn't have anything against brothers who showed off their feminine side. They just weren't my style or my bedroom taste. I considered myself a man's man, and that's what I wanted in my bed—a man who everyone in the room, male and female, was lusting over.

As I ran through my list of potential bed partners, I stopped at Randy Gonzales. Randy was a married army officer assigned to Fort Lee Army Base. He was a Dominican brother I'd met at Buffalo Wild Wings in Colonial Heights. Like most brothers on the DL, his wife didn't have a clue about Randy's bisexuality. Little did she know her soldier husband took the expression "don't ask, don't tell" to a whole new level. We'd hooked up only once, about a month ago, but I liked Randy. He was one cool guy with some pretty good dick. I thought about making him one of my sponsors, but the problem was he showed some signs of being obsessive. He'd been blowing up my phone nonstop for the past few weeks. Sure, I talked to him when he called, but I'd blown him off when he asked to hook up again. I'm sorry, but I don't do clingy. Not since the last obsessive, clingy motherfucker I messed with ended up becoming a stalker. But we'll talk about him a little later.

Right now, it was time to call my Latin bed warmer. He was too eager for me to let him become a regular, but his bedroom skills were just what I needed to cheer me up for the night. I clicked the TALK button on my phone. Randy had made it clear I could call anytime, day or night, for a booty call, as long as I pretended to be his duty officer. So, he was about to get a call from Sergeant Rock—rock hard, that is.

"Hello." The angry voice sounded familiar, but it wasn't Randy. His voice was deep, with a hint of an accent, but he sounded young. I'm embarrassed to say I was a little jealous. Had Randy found some young boy toy to fuck with behind my back?

I was about to hang up when the man on the other end said, "I know it's you, Jerome. I can see your number on my caller ID. Why the fuck you playing games?"

A knot formed in the pit of my stomach when I recognized the voice. Shit, I was surprised I hadn't known it was him right away. How could I have forgotten? His name was Ron, and he was twenty years my junior. Things ended pretty badly between us, and we hadn't spoken in a long time. I must have hit his number instead of Randy's.

"Ahh, Ron, I didn't mean to call your number, man. I was trying to get someone else." I was surprised he hadn't hung up already.

Ron and I had broken it off, or rather he'd broken it off by trying to put his fist through my nose. Despite the fact that he'd given me the worst beating of my life, just hearing his voice brought back all the good times we'd had together. Other than what I had with Big Poppa, he was the closest I'd ever come to being in love. Unfortunately, it also reminded me of the last words he'd spoken after he punched me in the face: *There is no us, Jerome. There never was. I'm just trying to get my life back.*

I heard a hissing sound. Finally, Ron spoke up. "Jerome, what the fuck do you want? Didn't I tell you to leave me the hell alone? As if my life isn't fucked up enough as it is, I got to get a call from you, the man who started all my troubles."

"How you doing, Ron?" I know it was weak, but I didn't know what else to say. I was trying to offer friendship, in hopes it would open the door again—eventually. I figured if he really didn't want to talk, he'd hang up.

"How am I? I'm fucked up, that's what I am, and it's all because of you! You fucked up my life."

I hated to admit it, but in a way, he was right. I had fucked up his life, and I was sorry for it, but there was nothing I could do at this point. I couldn't give him back what he'd lost. If I could, I would have, but all I had to offer him was a phat ass and some hungry lips.

I wasn't really into young guys, but somehow I was drawn to him. We'd met in a D.C. club, and later that night, he'd ended up at my room. He'd never had sex with a man before then, and I can't lie; I turned his ass out.

I guess in a way he turned me out, too, because I felt like I was twenty-five again hanging out with him. He had the sweetest body, and when it came to sex, he was like the Energizer Bunny: He kept going and going. We had really become tight, and I ended up spending most of my free time up in D.C.

In public, of course, we were just two straight guys hanging out together. Ron was not ready to come out of the closet. You see, a year ago, Ron had been a promising freshman on the Georgetown basketball team. It was obvious to everyone who'd seen him play that with the right coaching, he had a real shot at becoming an NBA player. He had way too much on the line with his career to reveal his sexuality, and I had had no problem with keeping it a secret as long as he kept giving me his good loving.

As much as I loved Big Poppa, I had considered letting him go for Ron. We really could have had something special—until he showed up at my hotel room one night and nearly beat me to death. Not that I could blame him after I saw the pictures.

I still haven't figured out how he did it, but somehow Peter, this crazy white guy who'd been stalking me ever since I turned him out, followed us and took some pretty compromising pictures that he eventually sent to Ron's coach, his teammates, and his mother. Peter was determined to make me his at all costs, and unfortunately, Ron paid the ultimate price when his sexuality became public.

"Ron, I'm sorry. I was hoping that one day we could get past all of that," I said in a soothing tone. "At least be friends."

"Get past it? I'm ruined. I had to move back to Danville with my mother, Jerome, and everyone in D.C. knows about me now. Everywhere I went, people would whisper. My team members didn't even want to play with me anymore, and they damn sure didn't want to get undressed in front of me. I had to quit the team, give up my scholarship, and move back home." Ron's voice cracked, and he broke down crying.

Damn, I had no idea things had gotten that bad. I thought some time might help, but obviously he was still hurting.

"I don't even wanna be here anymore. I wish I were dead. I hate this life."

"Ron, you don't mean that. You're a young man. You have a lot to live for."

"Like what? What the hell do I have to live for? They took basketball from me. Without basketball, I got nothing. The only thing I've wanted in my life was to be an NBA player."

I didn't know what to say, so I said what was in my heart. "Ron, can I come and see you? I just want to talk to you. You sound like you could use a friend."

"I don't need your kind of friendship, Jerome." With that, he disconnected the call. I wanted to dial his number again but decided it was better to leave well enough alone. The last thing I wanted to do was inflict any more pain on Ron.

Michael

3

It was one of those dreary, overcast days, and for once it looked like the weatherman was going to get it right when he predicted rain. The only reason I'd walked into Marty's Pawnshop in the first place was because of the bird's-eye view the large picture window gave me of the office building across the street.

I'd been browsing through the aisles of preowned jewelry, electronics, and knickknacks for twenty minutes, wasting time until she left the building. I finally stopped in front of a row of showcases filled with handguns. My eyes fixated on a pearl-handled Derringer. I wasn't a gun guy, but the thought of having a gun was becoming more and more appealing.

"May I help you, sir?" a heavy-set, balding, white man asked. He walked down the aisle behind the showcase until he was right in front of me. My best guess was that he was Marty, the owner.

"Oh, no, I'm just looking," I replied. I was a little embarrassed to be standing in front of the weapons. I didn't want him to think I was some kind of loony or, worse, a crook. "Just trying to kill some time while I wait for a friend across the street."

"Kill some time. That's kinda funny coming from a man standing in front of a gun case." He laughed, but I didn't.

"How much is that one?" I pointed at the Derringer.

The man gave me a strange look. "I can let you have it for three hundred fifty. But you do realize all the guns in this showcase are placed here with a woman in mind, right?"

I think my dumbfounded expression gave me away. I felt pretty stupid.

"What exactly are you looking for in a gun? Is it a gift?" I shook my head, and he said, "Target practice, hunting, protection—"

Before he could finish his list, I repeated his last word. "Protection. I own my own business and sometimes carry a lot of cash."

He pointed at the Derringer. "Well, that'll do it if your name is Lulu, but a big, strapping fellow like yourself needs some more firepower. Come with me. I think I've got what you need right over here."

I followed him to another glass showcase a few feet away. He took out a key to open the security door on the counter. The guns were neatly lined up in a row, some large, some small, but all looked deadly.

He pulled out a black handgun that looked like a policeman's gun. "How about this baby? She's a Glock nine-millimeter semi-automatic. This baby will put down a mugger quick, fast, and in a hurry."

He tried to hand it to me, but I shook my head. "No, that's too big. I want something smaller—something I can keep in my pocket that will still get the job done if I need it to."

"Okay, I think I have exactly what you need." Marty put the Glock back in the case, then pulled out another gun. "This is a twenty-five-caliber semiautomatic, what they call a Saturday Night Special on the street." It was much smaller, probably about the size of my hand; however, it was impressive because it had a clip and was semiautomatic.

"What kind of firepower?" I asked.

"It'll get the job done, that's for sure, and with this bad boy in your pocket, you never have to worry about a thing." He handed it to me.

I held the gun in my hand, aimed it at the picture window, and imagined myself shooting it at the black Mercedes parked in front of the building across the street. Its barrel had a sleek, smooth, criminal feel, and I knew right away that this was the one. It was like an instant marriage between the two of us—a man and his piece. "How much?"

"It's used, so I'll take two hundred fifty."

I glanced out the window again. "I'll take it."

"Not for five days you won't. State of Virginia has a five-day waiting period on the sale of all firearms." Now that he'd mentioned it, I did remember hearing about something like that in the news a while back when that kid shot up all those people at Virginia Tech. He took the gun off the counter and handed me some paperwork.

I filled it out and paid for the gun. By the time I was finished, I'd just about killed the forty minutes I'd wanted to waste. "I'll be back next week to pick it up."

"Thanks for your business." Marty shook my hand. "I'll see you next week."

It was raining lightly as I left the pawnshop. I walked over to my car, reached in for my umbrella, and opened it just as Loraine walked out of the building. I stood there mesmerized, watching her for a few seconds. To me, she was the most beautiful woman I'd ever seen. Hell, I'd been lusting after her since I was a teen, when she would come to my house to hang out with my older sister. Now she was the woman I'd fallen in love with, the woman I didn't want to lose, whether or not she was married.

I walked with purpose toward her car, determined to reach her before she had a chance to leave. She got there first, but I blocked the door with my leg before she could open it. She had a scowl on her face that actually surprised me.

"Hey, beautiful, long time no hear from." She'd always liked it when I called her beautiful, but this time it didn't have a positive effect on her. In fact, the way she was looking around all paranoid, it appeared to have had the opposite effect.

"Michael, what are you doing here?" she asked through gritted teeth.

I smiled. "Well, I hadn't heard from you in quite a while, so I figured I'd come see you. I miss you."

The beginnings of a smile crept up on her face. "I miss—" She stopped herself, glancing around, but it was too late. Now I knew she hadn't forgotten what we had.

"I knew it," I said with excitement before she could speak. "I knew you missed me." I leaned in to kiss her, but she turned her head and my lips landed on her cheek. Was she playing hard to get? If so, I was a patient man. The first step was already accomplished, getting her to admit she missed me.

"Michael, stop it." She actually sounded upset. This was more than just playing hard to get. "Do that again and I'm gonna slap you." She actually raised her hand as she said it.

"Stop what, Loraine?" I persisted. "Stop loving you? No can do. You might as well ask me to stop breathing."

Her whole body seemed to tense up, and she spoke to me in a low tone, as if she were worried someone might hear us. "Michael, please. You're embarrassing me." She reached for the door handle, but I stood my ground, only allowing her to open it a few feet.

"All right, then. Let's go somewhere we can talk." I stepped out of the way and let her get into her car. I would follow her once we agreed on a place to go. Or at least that's what I thought, until she made it clear our conversation was over.

"I'm not going anywhere with you. You know I'm trying to make it work with my husband."

I was trying to maintain some kind of composure, but when she mentioned her husband, I just blurted out my true feelings. "I don't give a shit about your husband. I love you, Loraine, and I'll do whatever it takes to make you mine."

She lowered her head. "I wish you didn't say things like that. I married him for better or for worse. You're just making things harder for us all."

"I know you're married. That has nothing to do with how I feel about you."

"Please, Michael, don't do this to me. We tried this already. I can't deal with seeing two men anymore. I'm tired of the lies, the sneaking . . ." She started glancing around again. Either she couldn't make eye contact with me, or she was afraid someone would come out of the building and see her talking to me.

"And me! You're tired of me, too, aren't you? You just used me, didn't you?" I stepped back from the car a bit, not really sure if I meant what I said or if I was just trying to get her riled up. She was too damn calm about our breakup.

"Michael, please don't talk that way. You're making this much harder than it should be."

"No, Loraine, you made this hard when you chose him over me!" I snapped.

"I don't have to listen to this." She placed the car in drive.

"No, please," I said desperately. "I'm not trying to piss you off. I just want to see you."

"Michael, you need to move on. I have."

"Have you?"

We both stared at each other silently until she said, "Yes, I have. I want you to also."

A punch in the stomach would have hurt a little less. "You don't know how I feel. I don't think I can move on. I love you, Loraine."

"Then I feel sorry for you, because I belong to someone else, and I'm not leaving him."

"Loraine, you can belong to whoever you want, but you know and I know that you're always going to be my woman."

"Michael, you're wroooong," she whined, dragging out the word *wrong* so much that it sounded more like *right* to me. "Good-bye, Michael. Don't come here anymore." She pulled off, and I watched her drive down the street.

"Bye, Loraine. I'll see you soon."

Leon

4

"Oh my goodness, I'm about to come," Loraine whispered, then suddenly she gasped, her back arched, and her body shook in small convulsions. "Oh, Michael . . . ," she moaned.

She thought I was asleep, but I could hear my wife masturbating next to me. It wasn't the first time. It had almost become routine—after we made love and she thought I was asleep, she'd play with herself until she climaxed. Talk about a blow to a man's ego; but it wasn't as if I could get mad at her about it, considering that twenty minutes ago I lasted only about two minutes tops. My doctor suggested I offer to go down on her, but Loraine was from the old school. Only thing she wanted sniffing around down there was my dick. Regrettably, I just couldn't deliver like I used to.

To make matters all that much worse, I'd just heard her moaning the name of that son of a bitch she had been fucking while we were separated. He was the subject of many an argument in my house. Not just because he was fucking my wife, who kicked me out when I hadn't even done anything wrong, but because my wife still cared about the guy. Oh, she denied it all the time, but I don't think she'd be moaning about a guy she didn't give a shit about. I mean, hell, I was lying in the bed next to her, for Christ's sake.

The idea that she might still feel something for this guy was not a surprise. I'd already found a stash of pictures and cards she'd been hiding in her closet. Women don't keep shit like that unless they aren't ready to let go of the memories. They keep the love notes around for those times when they want to reminisce.

You should have seen how pained she looked when I made her throw them out.

I lay there for a while until Loraine's breathing slowed down, and there was no more movement on her side of the bed. When she turned onto her left side, her favorite sleeping position, I curled up behind her until we were spooning. I wish I could say I drifted peacefully off to sleep, cuddled against my loving wife, but my mind just wouldn't let go of the fact that she'd cried out Michael's name. I loved my wife so much and was thankful that despite my shortcomings, she loved me too. But how much longer was she going to put up with a man who wasn't satisfying her? Especially when the other dude was apparently so good at giving her what she needed that she was still fantasizing about him?

At this point, I had two choices. I could either lie awake all night and worry, or I could be up front with Loraine. After a year in therapy with Roberta, I knew which one I had to do.

"Big Sexy, you asleep?" I shook her shoulder. There was silence for about ten seconds. She didn't even breathe, which told me she was awake, just surprised that I was also. She was probably wondering if I had heard her. I shook her again. "Loraine, you up?"

"I am now," Loraine said groggily. "What's with you? Can't sleep?"

"That guy Michael. When was the last time you seen him?"

She didn't answer my question until I nudged her from behind. "I don't know, Leon. I told you last week it's been a while. Why?"

"I heard you next to me. You called out his name."

"Oh, my." She fell silent. If she hadn't already figured out that I knew about her masturbating, there could be no doubt now.

Neither one of us spoke for a long time. I lay in the dark and stared at the ceiling, wondering what was going through my wife's head. Would she try to deny that she was thinking about him? I didn't know how I would handle it if she did. I mean, the average brother would already be going off on his woman if she called out someone else's name. I almost felt like I had to cut her some slack, though, because I knew I wasn't holding things down in the bedroom. But if she tried to deny it now, I just might have to get loud. I really didn't want to. Ever since we'd gotten back together, we were both trying hard to deal with things through talking instead of yelling.

"I'm sorry, Leon." She rolled over to face me. "I'm so embarrassed that you caught me masturbating. It's just that sometimes you finish so fa—"

I put my finger over her mouth in a hurry. No reason to hear her reminding me that I'd put in yet another minute-man performance. She hadn't exactly owned up to the fact that Michael was in her fantasy, but my ego couldn't handle the conversation if it was going to focus on me and my inadequacy.

"Look, Loraine, I know things still aren't great in that area of our marriage, but I'm working on it."

"I know you are, baby." She leaned in and kissed me. "And I'm so glad that you are. I know it wasn't easy for you to start seeing a therapist, but it means a lot to me that you've stuck with it. It tells me how much you care about making our marriage work."

"I do. I really do care. It's all I want, babe, for you and me to get back to the way we were in the beginning." I planted a kiss on her lips. "Speaking of therapy, the doctor wants me to consider trying hypnosis again. She thinks she can finally get to the root of my problem. She thinks it might have something to do with my aunt."

Loraine sat up in the bed. "You sure? Last time she hypnotized you, you almost had a breakdown. You barely get through the dreams now. This just might make things worse."

"Maybe, but there's a good chance it will make things better." I took her hand. "Whatever is wrong with me, I'm going to figure it out and fix it. We've been through some very tough times together, but somewhere in this cloud there's a silver lining. I'm just asking you to be patient until I find it."

Loraine wrapped her arms around me. "Leon, I love you more than anything in the world. I'm not going anywhere."

Jerome

5

I was sitting in Outback Steakhouse, sipping on a beer and checking out the menu when Freddie Coleman—or as I called him, my Thursday afternoon sponsor—walked into the restaurant. I gave him the once-over, checking him out from head to toe before I waved him over to our booth. Freddie was a short, dark-skinned man in his midthirties and was built like a brick shithouse. As always, he had a fresh cut and was meticulously dressed in a designer suit accessorized by tasteful gold and diamond jewelry. He'd made a small fortune in the computer software industry, and he wanted everyone to know it. I loved watching when he entered a room, because he reminded me of a modern-day George Jefferson. Freddie didn't walk; he strutted for everyone to see. I'd turned him out about a year ago, and we'd been meeting here at the Outback Steakhouse every Thursday afternoon since because of its close proximity to the Comfort Inn across the street.

"Jerome, how you doing, my man?" He smiled, giving me a fist bump before taking the seat across from me.

"I'm good, Freddie. Trying to keep busy. How about you? You're looking sharp as ever."

He grinned, brushing off his sleeves. "Thanks, man. The suit's Armani. Damn thing cost me more than my house note."

"Wow, you really balling, aren't you? Business must be good."

"Business is good, man. Thanks for that tip about those city contracts going up for bid. I been trying to get with the city for quite a few years. Where do you be finding all this stuff out?"

I leaned in close and whispered, "If I told you, I'd have to kill you, and then who would I have sex with every Thursday afternoon?"

I ran my tongue across my lips in a mischievous smirk. As dark as he was, I could see Freddie blushing as he looked around at the people dining nearby.

"Man, you gotta stop doing that. Somebody might see you." Like most of the men I messed with, Freddie was married and very paranoid about getting caught cheating on his wife with a man. Rumor had it he had a very jealous, very vociferous wife who loved to make a scene.

"Calm down. Nobody's going to see us. And so what if they do? Two black men can't have a business meeting in a restaurant? It's not like I'm sucking your dick for everyone to see."

I laughed because he was blushing again. "You right, man. I just get this feeling someone has been watching me recently. And my old lady's been acting real suspicious lately—like she knows something but ain't got no proof. You know what she asked me the other day? She asked me if I'd ever slept with a man."

I sat back in my seat. "Get the hell outta here. What'd you say?" I loved to listen to the lies these fools told their wives, trying to slide their way out of being gay. I swear, some of the shit they came up with was ingenious.

"I said to her, 'No, I haven't. Not unless you've changed your name to Jerome.' Then I said, 'Why? That one of your fantasies—to see me with a man'?"

We both burst out laughing. "You actually said that to her?"

"Uh-huh, I sure did."

"Man, I swear you got a pair of balls on you."

He leaned in and said, "You would know, wouldn't you?"

"Better than most, but maybe I should do a little more personal inspection. I think they've gotten bigger since the last time I checked," I answered with a wink.

"Maybe you should, but before that, I got a surprise for you." He reached into his jacket pocket and retrieved a box that he handed to me.

"What's this?"

"Open it and find out."

My eyes widened when I opened it and saw a Rolex. I didn't even want to think about how much it cost. I was just praying it was real. Last time a guy gave me a Rolex, it turned out to be a knockoff.

"Wow! I don't know what to say." I kept staring at it. This was not a cheap gift.

"Just say thanks, man."

I tried on the watch, still a little awestruck at the extravagance of this gift. I expected to be taken care of, but this was one of the most expensive gifts I'd ever gotten in my life. He didn't know it, but he was about to get the dick sucking of his life when we got over to the hotel.

"Thanks. What did I do to deserve this?"

"A lot, but let's just call it a birthday present."

"My birthday isn't for another few months. Is that all it's for?"

"It's for all the good things you do for me. I can't begin to tell you how much these Thursday afternoons have meant to me." His eyes were shiny, like he might have been trying to hold back tears. "I'm just trying to repay you. You've shown me a side of myself that I've kept hidden for way too long. For once in my life, I feel like I can breathe."

I had never seen Freddie so emotional, and while I definitely didn't love the guy, I was moved by his generosity and his sudden vulnerability. I reached across the table and took his hand. To my surprise, he didn't pull away; it was like the other people in the room had become invisible to him.

"Listen, I've already got the room key. How about if we skip lunch and get straight to dessert?"

He gave me "the look," the one that let me know when he was ready for an afternoon of hot, steamy sex before he went back to the boring world of married life with two small children. "Man, you ain't said nothing but a word. Let's go," Freddie agreed, squeezing my hand.

As we stood up to leave, this tall, big-boned sister came rushing at us from the front of the restaurant. I didn't know the woman, but it was pretty obvious Freddie did when he said, "Oh, shit, that's my wife."

"I knew it! I knew! I knew you was messing with someone!" she screamed. "And it's a man! Oh my goodness, it *is* a man! Aw, hell no. I'ma kill your little black ass when I get you home!"

For all his flashiness and bravado, Freddie turned into a little bitch when his wife ran up on us. "Baby, baby, please. It's not what you think! This is just a business meeting."

Of course, you know his wife didn't want to hear that shit. She swung her oversized Coach bag, hitting him in the head like purse-swinging was some type of new martial art and she was a seventh-degree black belt. I don't know what she had in that bag, but I could see the knot swelling up on Freddie's forehead in a matter of seconds. He looked scared to death, and he wasn't waiting for another blow to connect. In a flash, he was out. I'd never seen anyone move that fast, but believe it or not, her big ass was right on his tail.

"Baby, stop, please! Baby, baby, please," he muttered, ducking and dodging the purse as he ran around the island of booths. "Jerome, will you please tell this woman that this is just a business meeting!"

"What you gonna do, you little sissy?" She stopped for a split second and turned to me. This woman was as tall as me and almost twice my size—and I weigh two hundred twenty pounds. The way she was looking at me and breathing all heavy like a raging bull reminded me of one of my new personal rules: Stay the hell out of other people's domestic battles; it's safer that way. I'd come to that conclusion last year after my attempts to get Loraine to leave her husband ended up with me being the bad guy, not to mention losing my job and my best friend. In this particular case, Freddie's linebacker wife was so mad I just might lose my life.

So, I glanced over at Freddie and said, "Man, I'm sorry, but you on your own."

"That's what I thought," she screamed, then took off after poor Freddie again. It got to the point where I just sat down in the booth again, shaking my head when I heard the people at a nearby table commenting that the two of them looked like a new version of Laurel and Hardy's comedy show.

"You think you can make a fool outta me? I don't think so!"

she shouted, continuing to pound Freddie over the head. She finally grabbed pooped-out Freddie by the collar, smacking him up a few times before dragging him out of the restaurant. Damn, I'd seen ass whippings before, but that was one for the decades. I guess I wouldn't be seeing Freddie again anytime soon. Oh well, at least I still had the Rolex on my wrist.

"Why didn't you help your little friend?" I heard a familiar voice and froze. He sounded so smug and self-satisfied; I had no doubt that his presence at the scene of this fiasco was no coincidence.

I looked in the direction of the voice, wishing I was just imagining things, but there he was: my worst nightmare, the man who'd caused so much drama in my life. His name was Peter, and he was a freelance investigative reporter for most of the central Virginia newspapers. I'd turned his ass out about a year and a half ago, and he'd been stalking me ever since. I put it on his ass so good the fool packed his shit and moved out on his wife and kids to be with me.

The crazy thing is we'd had sex only once. Don't get me wrong; I had a good time with him, and this white boy was real easy on the eyes. He looked just like George Clooney, but he was talking some old crazy-love shit. He wanted us to go up to Massachusetts, where gay marriage is legal, and get married. I tried to tell him nicely that it wasn't that type of party, but he didn't want to hear it. I really think he snapped, and for the last year and a half, he'd been using his investigative skills and resources to ruin my relationships.

"You told his wife where to find us, didn't you?"

Peter nodded, looking smug as he slid into the booth to sit across from me. "You're a creature of habit, Jerome."

"Why are you doing this to me?"

"Let's not play stupid, all right? You know why I'm doing this. And you know how to stop it."

"Can't you see I don't want you?"

"That's because you're not trying to want me. I told you before, if I can't have you, nobody will. I mean that, Jerome. Eventually, I'm going to be the last man on Earth when it comes to your choices in men. And we both know Tiger Woods ain't got shit on you when it comes to sexual addiction." He laughed hard.

"You're stalking me. I'm gonna go to the police."

"Didn't you try that once before? How did that work out for you?"

"Fuck you!" When I had gone to the police, they told me he had done nothing that I could press charges for. Either he was just a really smart stalker, or the guy had connections with the department, because those cops practically laughed me out of their precinct.

He had the audacity to pick up my beer and take a swig. "That's exactly what I want you to do. You know, if you *were* fucking me, you wouldn't have all these problems. What d'you say? I saw you go over there and get a room. Why don't we put it to good use? No need for you to waste good money."

"Any chance you ever had is gone." The glare I gave him was laced with so much hate that if looks really could kill, Peter would have turned to dust right there on the spot. "So leave me the fuck alone."

"I can't leave you alone. I'm in love with you. So get used to me, 'cause I'll be around a lot more."

I stood up to leave, and Peter threw one last question my way.

"Oh, by the way, is Freddie Big Poppa?"

Peter had been trying to figure out who Big Poppa was ever since this stupid receptionist at my former job let the cat out of the bag that someone named Big Poppa was very important to me. It was probably driving Peter's super-sleuth ass crazy that he hadn't been able to dig up anything on Big Poppa, but I'd done everything I could not to let it happen.

Living in a gated community definitely helped. The guards at the booth had a photo of Peter, with specific instructions that he was never to be let into the neighborhood. We never went out in public together, and Big Poppa let himself into my neighborhood with his own key, so it pretty much left Peter at a dead end. Still, as good as Peter had been at exposing so many of my other lovers, I knew I had to remain cautious. This was my opportunity to take Peter off the hunt for Big Poppa.

"Yes," I said with a dramatic sigh. "You outed Big Poppa. Are you happy?"

"If you're going to lie, at least make it convincing," he scoffed. "I'm gonna find out who he is sooner or later, Jerome. And when I do, your world is going to come crumbling down."

My lie didn't work, so I resorted to threats. "Peter, you keep messing with me, and all you gonna do is end up dead."

"As long as you're lying beside me, Jerome, my life will have been complete."

I left the restaurant knowing that it was only a matter of time before I'd be hearing from Peter again.

Leon

6

I sat back in my chair, nervously tightening my grip on Loraine's hand when Roberta walked into the room. This wasn't one of my usual Thursday afternoon sessions with my shrink. No, today was the day she was going to hypnotize me. I was dreading it, but I knew it was important that I try to get to the bottom of my issues if I wanted to keep my marriage.

Roberta turned and smiled at my wife. "Hey, Loraine. I didn't know you were going to be joining us today."

"Well, Dr. Marshall, considering what happened last time he was hypnotized, I thought I'd better be here for moral support." Loraine let out a sigh. "I tried to explain to Leon that if you're hypnotizing him just because of our problems in the bedroom, you don't have to do this. I can live with our sex life the way it is. I love my husband. I don't want him traumatized. He can barely deal with the dreams of his uncle beating his ass as it is."

"I appreciate what you're saying, Loraine, I really do, but this decision is not about you or me. It's about Leon. Ultimately he has to decide if he wants to know his past or not, because without that knowledge, he can't move forward."

Loraine looked at me and patted my hand. "You don't have to do this. We'll be okay."

I was happy that she'd come with me. She'd really stood by me when other women wouldn't have, but no matter what she said, no wife could deal with this forever. "Yeah, I do. You can say whatever you want, but how long are you gonna be happy with half a man? I need to know why this is happening to me, Loraine. I need to know why I'm behaving the way I am so the doctor can help me figure out a way to fix it. I can't live like this."

"Well, with that being said, are you ready?" Dr. Marshall gave me an encouraging smile.

"Yeah, I'm as ready as I'll ever be." I glanced at my wife, almost hating to let go of her hand. My legs trembled, but I knew I had to go forth and face this challenge. If I didn't fix my problems, I would never be the man this wonderful woman I married deserved.

"Loraine, I think it will be a little easier for Leon to concentrate if you're not in the room. The slightest distraction and he may not go under."

Loraine glanced at me, and I nodded. "Okay, but, Leon, honey, if you need me, I'll be right outside the door."

"I know, Big Sexy, and I love you for it."

"I love you too."

I watched my wife walk out the door, then sat halfway back in the chair, trying to relax. I still didn't understand how this whole hypnotism thing worked, but it sure as hell did work, and that creeped me out. Maybe some memories were better off left buried.

Roberta dimmed the lights, then walked over and sat in the chair next to me. "Just relax, Leon. Loosen your hands. Take a deep breath," she began in a slow, soothing voice. I unclasped my hands, which I hadn't realized were clenched into fists. "Sit back in the chair. Let it recline until you're comfortable."

I did as I was told. I felt like I was standing on the edge of a steep cliff, not knowing whether I should jump. It was now or never. I couldn't go on the way I was living.

"Do you remember how we did this last time?" she whispered.

"Uh-huh." How the hell could I forget? I could still feel the sting from the strap my uncle used to beat the crap out of me. It was something I had successfully blocked out of my psyche until we unearthed it during hypnosis, but now it would never leave me. I was terrified knowing that I might be preparing to dredge up some more painful memories now.

She began speaking slowly. "I want you to listen to my voice. Block out everything but my voice. Can you do that?"

I nodded my head.

"Good. Now, I want you to close your eyes. . . . Take deep, slow breaths. . . . Relax . . ."

I closed my eyes and tried to slow my breathing.

"Now, we're going to go on a little trip back in time. A happy trip to see your aunt Barbara. You want to see your aunt Barbara, don't you? You want to relive those good times you shared, right?"

"Yeah."

"Good. Now, I want you to count backward slowly with me, starting at ten."

"Ten . . . nine . . . eight . . . seven . . ." We spoke in unison. By the time I made it to one, I was completely relaxed.

"Leon, can you hear me?" Roberta's voice sounded like a faint echo.

"Yes, I can hear you, but you seem so far away."

"That's okay. Just listen to my voice. I want you to think about your aunt," Roberta's voice droned on. "I want you to think about a time she made you happy. Your mind should be clearer now. You should be able to remember. Now, go back in your mind and think of a happy time with your aunt."

All of a sudden, I was thirteen again. My body was hurting me all over, and I could feel the welts on my back starting to swell from the leather strap my uncle had beaten me with. He was cursing my name while I cowered in a corner, waiting for the next blow. It never came, because from out of nowhere, Aunt Barbara threw her body in front of me, shielding me from his wrath. She'd never done that before, and I was both thankful and surprised.

"Leave this boy be, Charles! You gonna kill him with that strap."

"Better he be dead than tell me no to anything," my uncle shouted. "Now, you can stand in the way if you want to, but he best have that yard work done before I get home."

Yard work! Was that what this was all about? He woke me

out of my sleep and damn near beat me to death because I didn't cut the grass.

The door slammed a few seconds later, and my aunt said, "Come here, baby. You okay? He didn't hurt you again, did he?" I tried to hold back tears, but it didn't work. Once I saw Aunt Barbara's tears, the water works were unstoppable. For ten minutes, we held each other and cried.

"I hate him," I finally yelled.

"*Hate* is a very strong word," my aunt said. She got up and walked to a cupboard, bringing back a familiar jar filled with a white cream. "You don't hate him."

"I do. I hate him."

"Don't say that, Leon. Your uncle loves you. He just has a strange way of showing it sometimes."

"If that's what love is, I don't want it. One day you'll wake up and I'm gonna be gone."

Aunt Barbara frowned like I'd hurt her feelings. "Would you really leave your auntie, Leon? Don't you know you all I got in this world? I'd rather be dead than be without you, boy."

"I'm sorry, Auntie, but if he keeps beating me like this, I have to leave. I've got no reason to stay—unless I want him to kill me."

She turned me around and began tenderly applying the cream to the welts on my back one by one, and with each one, I felt myself relaxing.

"Thank you."

"You're welcome, baby. Just make me one promise."

"What is it?"

"Please don't leave me."

"I can't promise that, Aunt Barbara. That man means to kill me." No matter how kind she was, I didn't know how much more of my uncle's abuse I could take. It wasn't just the beatings. The man was a control freak who wouldn't let me off the property. Sometimes I felt like a slave put on Earth to cater to him.

Aunt Barbara was quiet for a while as she gently stroked my back. Finally, she spoke so quietly I almost didn't hear her.

"Well, then, baby, I guess I'm gonna have to give you a reason to stay." She placed a hand on my shoulder and turned me around.

When I faced her, Aunt Barbara took me in her arms and kissed me on the mouth. At first, it felt like an innocent kiss, like when she would peck me on the lips before I left for school. But then, all of a sudden, she pushed her tongue into my mouth. This felt strange. I'd never kissed a woman before that, never even thought about it. All I cared about was playing ball and riding my bike.

I was old enough to know that what she was doing was not something an aunt usually did with her nephew. I thought for a moment that I should stop her, but this was Aunt Barbara, and I trusted that she would never do anything that would hurt me. Besides, while my mind was trying to process what was happening, my body had begun to respond, and it was feeling good. Before I knew it, I started tonguing her back, and we were kissing passionately like I'd seen people doing on the soap operas.

When we broke the kiss, my penis was as stiff as a board and she smiled at me in a way that made me feel like a man, not her nephew. I wasn't really sure how I felt about that and was glad when she sent me to my room to get ready for school.

That's when I heard Roberta's faraway voice calling me.

I opened my eyes and looked around. I was disoriented, but I was no longer at Uncle Charles and Aunt Barbara's house. "Where am I?"

"You're safe," Roberta said. "You're in my office."

I was looking for Aunt Barbara. I couldn't believe what I'd just recalled, but I knew it was true that that was how things had happened.

"You okay? Do you remember what happened?" Roberta could see I was a little flustered.

"Oh my God. Yeah, I remember what happened . . . but I'm not sure I want to believe it."

"What do you mean?"

"My uncle was always physically abusing me, and my aunt was always my comforter, my protector. But there's something else." I stopped myself from explaining further. It wasn't like I could just blurt out the fact that I'd just relived my very first kiss with a woman, and the woman turned out to be my aunt. Even if she wasn't my blood relation, it just wasn't right.

"What is it, Leon?"

"I think I know why I like big women, but I don't want Loraine to know."

Michael

7

I hurried out of Marty's Pawnshop just as Loraine reached the sidewalk in front of her office building. It was only a little after four, and she usually didn't leave the office until sometime after five. Thankfully, I'd spotted her through the picture window just as Marty and I were finishing up my gun transaction. Once again, I was hoping to get her to sit down and talk to me. I was sick without her, and I knew in my heart that if I could just get her alone for ten minutes, I could convince her that we should be together. Unfortunately, I quickly found out I wouldn't be getting the chance to talk to her at all, because just as I was about to cross the street, Leon pulled up in a black Mercedes truck.

Dammit! What the hell was he doing here? It was Thursday. Wasn't he supposed to be at his shrink's office in a half hour? After sneaking around with Loraine for the better part of a year, I probably knew Leon's schedule better than he did. From his Tuesday and Thursday therapy sessions to his Saturday night poker games and his Sunday morning golf outings, I always knew when Loraine would be free of him, at least until now.

I thought my blood would boil as I watched her get in his truck and lean in for a kiss. She kissed him deeply, just like she used to do to me when I'd pick her up for one of our many rendezvous. I wanted to run across the street and confront them both, but then I realized that once they saw me, all Leon had to do was pull away from the curb and I'd be left standing there like a fool. Instead, I turned around and walked to my car. I drove around the corner so I could follow them.

The first stop they made was at Leon's shrink's office, where they both got out and stayed a little more than an hour. I guess they were doing some type of couples counseling. Leon didn't look too good when they came out, and I was surprised when Loraine jumped in the driver's seat.

A few minutes later, instead of heading home, they got onto I-64 east. I hung back about five cars behind them for twenty-five minutes, wondering where the hell they were going. By that time, I wasn't even sure why I was following them in the first place. I was actually embarrassed when it dawned on me that my behavior was bordering on obsessive. I wasn't that type of guy— at least I hadn't been before Loraine broke my heart.

I was just about to turn around when the signs indicated we were about fifteen miles outside of Williamsburg. That's when a knot formed in my stomach. I had a strong suspicion that I knew exactly where they were headed.

No, she wouldn't take him there. She wouldn't do that to me, would she?

I raced ahead of them, pulling into Kings Mill Resort and Spa a good five to ten minutes before they would—if I was right about their destination. I avoided the valet parking, which I knew Loraine would insist on, and pulled into the self-service parking lot. It gave me a clear view of the entrance to the main building. I was still holding out hope that they were going somewhere else, but I doubted it. Like me, Loraine loved everything about this place.

I'd found Kings Mill Resort and Spa online when we were dating. It was the first place we ever went overnight together. We'd spent many a romantic night curled up near the fireplace in our room or down in the spa getting couples massages and facials. This was our private little getaway spot, and we'd made a promise to each other that no matter what happened, we'd never take anyone else here. I guess I was the only one who took that promise seriously, because regrettably, Leon's black truck pulled up to the valet not long after I arrived.

When they got out of the truck, Loraine was all over Leon, rubbing his back, leaning up against him with her head on his shoulders. I know they were married, but I felt so disrespected.

This was our spot, not theirs. Why the hell would she bring him here in the first place? Somehow, I kept it together, because it would have been so easy to drive right up to the valet station, pull out my new gun, and blow Leon's ass away. I singled out Leon because I don't think I could ever harm a hair on Loraine's head. I loved her too much for that.

A few minutes later, I watched as they walked into the lobby. I got out of my car and strolled to the entrance, trying to look casual, not like the crazy-jealous ex-lover I had become. Don't ask me what my next move would be, because I didn't have a clue. I did, however, have my gun in my pocket—just in case Leon wanted to give me a little trouble. By the time I reached the lobby, they'd checked in and were probably halfway to their room, so I sat down on one of the many sofas, determined not to leave until I made some kind of statement.

I sat there for about twenty minutes, trying to come up with a plan. It was hard, because my mind kept wandering, filled with memories of the visits Loraine and I had made to this place. Finally, I picked up the house phone and asked to be connected to Mr. and Mrs. Farrow's room.

"Hello." Leon answered the phone on the second ring.

I cleared my throat. "Afternoon, Mr. Farrow, this is the front desk. Can I please speak to your wife?"

"Sure. Hold on."

That was easier than I expected. He didn't even sound suspicious about why the front desk would need to speak to Loraine and not him. Maybe they had checked in under her name. After all, she was the major breadwinner in that household, and it did seem that she wore the pants in the relationship. When Loraine came on the line, though, I understood why Leon wasn't surprised, and it was not for the reason I thought.

"Well, that was fast," she said. "I just called down a few seconds ago. I was hoping to schedule a couple's massage."

I paused for a beat, feeling the jab of her words. She was scheduling a massage for her and Leon. This was a romantic weekend, all right, but as far as I was concerned, she was with the wrong man. I realized I better speak up quickly or my chance would be lost. "I'd love to schedule you for a massage. Oh, and

I just happen to have an opening right now. Why don't you come down to the lobby so we can get started right away?"

She didn't answer immediately. I hadn't made any effort to disguise my voice, so she was probably in shock once she realized who she was speaking to. The fact that she didn't immediately hang up on me gave me hope and made me feel bold.

"You can leave your husband upstairs. Our couples massages are sold out."

"I see . . . ," she said, and then her voice trailed off like she had no idea what to say, especially with Leon standing in the room, probably right next to her.

"Why don't you come down to the lobby . . . or should I come up to your room?"

She finally found her voice. "No, no. I'll be right down with another credit card for you."

"I'll be waiting." I hung up the phone feeling satisfied.

I saw Loraine step off the elevator. From the look on her face, it was clear that she was nowhere near as happy to see me as I was to see her. Loraine's eyes searched the lobby until she found me sitting on the sofa. She had this tigress look, as if she could tear me apart with her bare hands. I actually found it rather sexy, to be honest with you. Lord, what I would do to have her hands pawing all over me.

She pointed at me and then gestured for me to follow her as she walked down a corridor away from the lobby. I did as I was told, watching her large hips sway as I walked behind her. When she stopped at the end of the hallway, she spun around and all but pounced on me as she talked through clenched teeth. "What the hell is wrong with you? Do you know my husband is upstairs?"

"Sure do. What I wanna know is what's he doing here?" I retaliated with equal venom. "How dare you bring him here? This is supposed to be our place. First you crush my dreams; now you're taking them away. How could you do me like this?"

"Do you like what? What the hell did I do to you? I'm married, for Christ's sake. Which part of that don't you understand?"

"What I understand is that you love me! That you can't look

me in the face and tell me that you don't. That you're afraid to be around me because you're afraid of how it makes you feel." I took a step closer to her, and she took two steps back.

"Is that what it's gonna take for you to leave me alone? Well, all right, then, look me in my face." She stepped up and grabbed me by my shirt, forcing me to look at her. "I don't love you, Michael. I don't want you, and right now I don't even like you. Now will you leave me alone?"

"Please, you don't mean that. You're just upset." I had to play it cool, like her words didn't faze me, when in reality, I felt like I was dying inside.

"Damn right I'm upset. If I had known you'd end up following me around, acting like a stalker, I would have never messed with you in the first place."

My mind flashed briefly on the concealed weapon I was carrying, and I wondered if maybe I had become everything she was accusing me of. But I couldn't believe that about myself. I wasn't a stalker; I just knew that no matter what she said, we were meant to be together. I tried to soften my tone. "I'm not a stalker, Loraine. I just want to talk to you."

"Well, I don't wanna talk to you. Now, I've got to get back with my husband," Loraine said, pivoting on her foot to leave.

I reached out and yanked her back toward me, surprising even myself. "Loraine, don't do this. Talk to me." I didn't mean to hold her arm so tightly, but I needed her to listen.

"Get your hands off me!" Loraine looked down at my hand and glared at me. She snatched her arm away. "I'm going to say this one time and one time only: Stay the hell away from me! Do I make myself clear?"

"Would you rather I come back up to your room with you? If you think I'm going to let you and Leon defile our relationship, you better think again."

The first time, this threat had brought her out of her room to come talk to me, but it didn't work twice.

"Michael," Loraine said, eyes narrowed in defiance, "you come to our room and I swear to God I'll call security and have you locked up. Now, it's time you moved on with your life."

"Loraine, I'm not giving up on you or our love. We're meant to be together."

"You know what, Michael? You're starting to scare me."

"Scare you? Is Leon putting these thoughts in your head? I would never hurt you."

"No, he's not putting these thoughts in my head. If anyone's putting them in my head, it's you, Michael, by your actions."

"So you really feel like I'm stalking you?"

"What do you call a man who sits outside his ex-girlfriend's job unannounced? I saw you come running out of the pawnshop when I came out of the building today. I've also seen you drive around my cul-de-sac at all hours of the night. Now you show up here. So if you're not stalking me, what the hell are you doing? 'Cause whatever it is, it sure ain't healthy."

"I'm not stalking you; I just want to see you. Is that so bad?"

"How many times do I have to tell you? I don't want to see you, Michael. I'm not going to ruin my marriage for a hopeless affair. What we had is over. Can you please get that through that thick skull of yours? Now stay away from my job, my house, and me. If you come around me again, I'll call the police on you."

"Loraine, I don't care what you say. I know you love me."

It took her a moment to answer, but she finally said, "A woman can't love two men, Michael."

With that, Loraine stormed off, leaving me standing alone. For the first time, I noticed a few people in the hallway, milling around as if they had been watching the whole thing.

"Mind your own business," I snapped at the gawking onlookers, then stalked out to my car. I really loved Loraine and wanted her back, but obviously I was going about it the wrong way. I would have to go home and come up with another plan.

Jerome

8

You ever hear the phone ring and just get a feeling you shouldn't answer it? Well, that's exactly how I felt when I heard the old-school ring tone signaling that someone was calling me from a restricted or private number. I almost never answer blocked calls, because it was usually my crazy-ass stalker Peter calling to harass me.

The only reason I was reaching for my phone was because of the off chance it was Big Poppa calling from his house phone to apologize for the shit he pulled recently. I had finally convinced him that we needed to start spending time together outside of my house—hell, outside of my bedroom. I needed him to prove that, after all this time together, I was more than just a fuck to him. He had never agreed to go anywhere outside the gates of my community, and whether or not it meant ducking my crazy stalker to do it, I needed a date with Big Poppa to prove that our relationship was deeper than just the physical.

Big Poppa agreed to go to the movies with me, but on one condition. He chose a theater way the hell out in Fredericksburg to be sure that we wouldn't run into anyone who knew him. Well, I was so happy to finally be going out somewhere with him that I didn't even complain. Besides, it gave us the opportunity to take a crazy-long route to get there so that if Peter did happen to be following us, we could lose him along the way.

We reached the theater pretty certain that Peter was not around—I guess even stalkers take a day off once in a while—but Big Poppa's plan to stay anonymous almost backfired on him in a big way. Would you believe he spotted a couple of his wife's friends in the lobby? This motherfucker got so nervous that he ducked out on me. While I was standing in line to buy popcorn, he told me he was going to the men's room, and that was the last I saw of him. The really messed up part about it was that he was the one driving, and I ended up stranded. Do you have any idea how much it costs to take a cab from Fredericksburg to the west end of Richmond? Eighty-one dollars and fifty cents, that's how much. I knew this because that's how much it cost me to get home. So it didn't matter which one it was—Big Poppa or Peter, either one of them was going to get a piece of my mind.

"Who is this?" I snapped.

"Jerome, I need your help, man." I recognized the voice right away. It wasn't Peter or Big Poppa; it was Ron, and he sounded distressed. I guess I thought him up, because he'd been weighing heavily on my mind since I called him by accident last week. Despite everything that had happened between us, I'd be fooling myself if I didn't admit I cared for the man and felt responsible for his well-being. Especially since the way he was talking about dying and wanting to be dead seemed more like a cry for help than anything else. So, if he really needed me, I was going to be there for him. I owed him that much, since it was my fault he got shoved out of the closet.

"Ron, what's the matter, man?"

"Jerome, I'm in trouble. I need your help bad." He sounded like he was on the verge of tears.

"Just tell me where you are and what you need."

"I need you to bail me out."

"Bail you out of what? You're not gambling, are you?" Ron liked to gamble. He'd shown me that side of himself the few times we'd snuck off to Atlantic City. But I'll tell you now, if he wanted me to pay off his gambling debts, he was ass out.

"No. They arrested me."

"Arrested you! Arrested you for what?"

"Assault. I had a fight with a guy. Can you just come down here and bail me out? You're the only one I can count on. They're gonna send me to County if I don't get bailed out soon."

Wow, I was blown away by what he'd said: I was the only one he could count on. I felt honored and a little guilty at the same time. I was pretty sure that before my stalker outed him, he had lots more people around who would have helped him. There was no way I could turn him down now. "Okay, I'm on my way. How much is your bail?"

"A thousand dollars," he said. My stomach tightened a little at the thought of putting out that much money. "But this guy just told me you can get a bail bondsman and it will cost you only fifteen percent."

"Don't worry. I'll take care of that. Where are they holding you?"

"Danville city jail."

"All right. I'm on my way."

I was relieved to hear I would have to pay only fifteen percent, but the truth was I would have paid the whole thousand if need be. Guilt, fondness, love . . . I didn't quite know how to define what I was feeling, but I definitely cared about Ron, and I wanted to be there for him in his time of need.

I'd just put my coat on and was about to head out the door when someone rang the doorbell. Without even looking through the peephole, I opened the door, and to my surprise saw Big Poppa standing there with a bottle of wine in one hand and a bag of groceries in the other. He had to pick now to apologize?

"Going somewhere?" he asked.

"I have to go help a friend."

"Well, I'll be here when you get back." He tried to step inside, but I blocked his way.

"No, you won't. I can't even believe you came over here after that shit you pulled. You didn't even call me and tell me you were leaving." I was pissed.

"Please, what did you expect me to do? Sit there and hold your hand? Those were two of my wife's friends, and I was supposed to be up in Charlottesville seeing my people. What the hell do you think they would think if they saw me sitting next to you sharing popcorn and a drink?"

"Nothing!" I said adamantly. "We were watching *Iron Man 2*, not *Brokeback Mountain*. You could have introduced me as your cousin. The least you could have done was circle back and pick my ass up."

"You know what, Jerome? You're right. I fucked up. I'm sorry, okay? I'm very, very sorry."

"Sorry ain't good enough this time." I reached for the door.

"Okay, then, how about this? Will this make it up to you?" He held up the bottle. "Your favorite wine. And guess what?" He showed me the bag of groceries, then winked at me. "I got the little scallops you like." He stepped closer to me. "I'm going to sauté them in a little olive oil, garlic, and butter and serve them over angel-hair pasta. And when we finish eating . . ." He smirked. "Well, do I have to say it? You know what I do best." He started swerving his hips like an exotic dancer.

Shit. I almost dropped my keys. You know I'd be lying if I said it didn't sound great. Big Poppa was a hell of a cook, and who doesn't know that there's no better sex than makeup sex?

"Seriously, Jerome, I'm sorry. Can you let me make it up to you?"

I bit my lip and silently cursed. Why was it I could never say no to this man?

Ah, what the hell. An hour for dinner, fifteen or twenty minutes for a quickie, and I could still be in Danville in three hours.

"You got a lot of making up to do. I hope you're up to the challenge."

He smiled broadly. "Challenge is my middle name."

I finally made it to the jail in Danville, only fifteen minutes before they shipped Ron over to County. I was thankful to have made it in one piece. Trust me, I'd pushed my poor Lexus to the limit to make the drive in a little less than two hours. I normally didn't like to drive that fast, but Big Poppa had me leaving my place much later than I expected when he turned what should have been a quick blow job and a good-bye into a mini-marathon. He must have sensed something was wrong, because he didn't leave my house until sometime after four in the morning. He rarely ever did that unless his wife was out of town, and believe me, I knew she was home.

Call me obsessed, but I always knew what his wife was up to.

Neither Big Poppa nor his wife knew it, but I kept track of their Facebook pages like they were my own. That woman friended me and she didn't even realize who I was. It's amazing just how careless people are about giving up their personal information on social networking sites like Facebook, MySpace, and Twitter. An hour before Big Poppa showed up at my door, she'd updated her status to say she was watching a Lifetime movie in her big, comfy bed. Chick movies—no wonder Big Poppa took the opportunity to get out of the house.

Speaking of Big Poppa, he was full of surprises tonight. As I was walking up to the window to pay Ron's bail, I received an unexpected call. Why the hell Big Poppa wasn't in bed snuggled up next to his wife by now, I don't know. Most of the time after we had sex, it took him a day or two to call me if I didn't call him first. I should have just hit the IGNORE button on my phone, but like I said before, I just couldn't say no to the man.

"Hello," I said groggily, as if I had been sleeping.

"Where the hell are you?" No mistaking his attitude; the man was pissed about something. I strolled toward the exit to continue the call outside, because it felt like this conversation was about to get serious.

"I'm . . . I'm—" I was about to say I was in bed, but I had my own suspicions about this call. Had he doubled back to my house and found I wasn't there? Jesus, I hoped not. "Why? Where are you?" I tried to throw it back at him.

"Jerome, don't play games with me. I called your house phone five times. I know you're not there. Now, where the hell are you?"

Shit! This was going to be a problem. While I was flattered that he was finally showing interest this way, why couldn't he have waited until I helped Ron straighten out his dilemma? I mean, I'd waited all this time for Big Poppa to show that he cared; another week wouldn't have hurt. I had to remain on the defensive.

"I stepped out for a minute. Is there a problem? What's up?"

"Stepped out! At six o'clock in the morning? Where the fuck are you? With some nigga?"

"No, not exactly. I'm helping out a friend." I tried to act like it was no big deal, but this was huge. Big Poppa and I had had our share of arguments, but I'd never heard the anger that I was hearing in his voice. He knew I had sponsors, and he'd never expressed jealousy before.

"Helping him out? How the hell you helping him out? With a blow job? I knew you were acting funny all night, trying to rush me out of there all fast and shit."

"Look, if it's any of your business, I'm bailing out a friend who got arrested." Hey, you know what they say: nothing better than the truth. Except that Big Poppa didn't believe it.

"You fucking liar. What's wrong? All of a sudden I ain't got what you need?"

"Don't go there, all right? You know how I feel about you. I'm not the one with a wife I go running home to every night."

"No, you're the one who risks both our lives with about fifteen different bed partners. Now, I want your ass home before I get there, or you can expect a foot in your ass."

Oh, no, he didn't just threaten to hit me! Look, I loved the guy, but who the hell did he think he was talking to? Now I was just as pissed off as he was.

"Excuse me? I know you're not talking to me, 'cause I wanna know what damn army you plan on bringing to help you get your foot in my ass. I think you're starting to take that Big Poppa shit a little too literally, wouldn't you say?" He was silent, so I continued. "And as far as me going home, you want me home, then pack your bags and move in, because I don't answer to anyone unless they sleep in my bed every night, and that damn sure ain't you."

"What you trying to say?"

"Think about it. You'll figure it out."

I hung up on him and then turned off my phone as I proceeded to the magistrate's window to pay Ron's bail.

I sat down and waited for him to be processed and released. The magistrate said his processing would take about a half hour, so I read an old newspaper someone had left on the bench. I hadn't gotten through half of it before I looked up and saw Ron walking down the corridor toward me.

The sight of him after all this time apart really stirred something inside me. I remembered his phenomenal body, but I'd completely forgotten just how handsome he was, and the closer he came, the more I wished I could just reach out and grab him. How the hell did I ever let this man out of my life? He looked like some kind of African god. A whole host of emotions rose up within me as he approached. So much had been going on in my life lately, with the loss of my best friend and my job, Peter's continual harassment of me and my friends, and now Big Poppa showing his ass. Seeing Ron made me long for the carefree times we had had together before things got so complicated. Big Poppa should be careful, I thought, because for the first time, I could imagine him being replaced.

By the time Ron was standing in front of me, my mind was swimming. I know it was shallow, especially after all that we'd been through, but all I could think of was that I wanted to sleep with this man again in the worst way.

"Thanks, Jerome," he said, his voice showing the innocence of his youth. He was almost twenty years my junior, but when I was around him, I was the one who felt like I was twenty.

"You don't have to thank me. I'm always going to be here for you." I stood up to hug him, but he took a step back.

"Don't . . . don't kiss me," he whispered, lifting his hand defensively as if he wanted not only me, but also everyone else in the building to see the invisible barrier between us. It was actually quite comical, because his words told one story, but his eyes told me something entirely different. He was checking me out, and there was no doubt in my mind that he was undressing me with his eyes. He wanted me. He just didn't want to be classified as gay.

"I wasn't gonna kiss you. I was just gonna shake your hand and give you a little embrace. Man, it's been a long time, but if you don't feel comfortable with that, I understand."

"Well, I don't feel comfortable."

I nodded my understanding.

"I do appreciate you coming down here and bailing me out and everything. I'm just trying to put all that other stuff behind me." I wanted to tell him that he couldn't put who he was behind him, but that was something he'd learn with time.

"That's the way you want it, that's the way it is. You hungry? My car's right outside. Let's go get something to eat."

He didn't reply. He just started walking to the door, and of course I followed.

Loraine

9

I ended up at Egypt's door in need of a friendly ear. Ordinarily I wouldn't show up at her house without calling, but I knew her husband was out of town on business. I also knew she had a bottle of my favorite wine, and, boy, I could use a drink or two.

When Egypt answered the door, I gave her a pitiful look and said, "Girl, I hope you don't mind, but right about now I could use a friend."

"Of course I don't mind. Come on in." She embraced me. "You all right? What's wrong? We missed you at book club last week."

"Please, with all this craziness going on in my life, I wasn't even thinking about book club," I said sadly as I walked past her into the house. "You still have that bottle of wine I brought over here last week for our book club meeting?"

"Yeah." She nodded. "It's in the bar fridge. Let me get it for you." She walked through her foyer and into the family room. I followed behind her and sat on one of the stools while she poured two glasses of wine.

"So, what's going on, girl? Everything all right at home?" she asked as she handed me a glass.

"Like I said before, I don't even know where to start. My life's so screwed up you'll probably end up thinking I'm insane by the time I finish telling you this story." I took a long swallow and drained nearly half the glass of wine.

She laughed. "Try me. I've been through my share of drama, remember?" I had to chuckle because she wasn't lying. My little bit of BS was nothing compared to what she and her sister went through last year. When Egypt asked her sister to carry a baby for her and her husband, who just happened to be her sister's ex, things got way out of control. They had so much drama somebody should have written a book about that shit. Nonetheless, I was there to vent about my own mess, so that's exactly what I did.

"Okay, well, Michael showed up outside my office the other day and followed me and Leon all the way down to Williamsburg."

"Michael? Who the hell is Michael?" She put her hand up to stop me. "Wait a minute. Michael . . . Michael . . . Why does that name ring a bell?" She was silent for a moment, and then her eyes got wide. "I remember him! That's the light-skinned pretty boy you took on the dinner cruise last Valentine's Day."

"Uh-huh, that's him." I didn't like the way she categorized him as a pretty boy. It made him sound stuck-up, and Michael was far from that. Because he'd spent his teenage years as the fat kid who couldn't get a date, he was actually pretty humble for someone who was now hotter than hot. I didn't protest Egypt's description, though, because I know she didn't mean any harm. She'd met Michael, and at the time, she didn't seem to think he was conceited. Besides, how would I look now, defending my ex when I had just recommitted myself to my marriage?

"Damn, I forgot about him. Girl, you sure had everybody whispering about you that night. I thought he was just something to do to get back at Leon while you were separated, but there was one rumor that he might have been a hired escort."

I sat back on my stool, truly offended. "Hell no, he's not an escort! Michael is my boo—" Oh, shoot. Had I really just said that? I wished I could take it back, but it was too late now. "Or at least he *was* my boo," I corrected myself. "I don't have to pay some man to be with me!" That kind of shit pissed me off. Some people seem to think that the only way a big sister can get a good-looking man is with her pocketbook. Just some jealous haters, as far as I was concerned. They had no idea how many men prefer a woman with a nice, soft body and some meat on her bones to press up against.

Egypt threw her hands up in the air. "Listen, don't kill the messenger. You know how petty them people at the office can be. They're always talking about someone. And nobody expected you to show up to a Valentine's Day party with a man other than Leon. Hell, me and you are pretty tight, and you didn't even tell me about him."

"That's 'cause I don't keep my business all out in the street." Egypt was about the closest thing I had to a female best friend, but I still kept most of my personal business personal, especially since she worked in my office, where nosy people would no doubt be pumping her for information. "But, anyway, when I got with Michael, I was done with Leon. At least until I found out my so-called best friend had set Leon up. Girl, I could still kill Jerome's ass for doing that shit." I didn't know if the pain of that betrayal would ever go away.

"Oh, Jerome . . ." She shook her head but left the subject alone. Egypt used to try to get me to reconcile with him, but fortunately she knew enough not to bother anymore. She brought the subject back to Michael. "I just didn't know things were so serious with this Michael."

"They were about as serious as you could get until I found out my husband never cheated on me." I took a sip of my wine. "That's why I'm in this predicament now."

"What predicament? Why didn't you just tell Michael that you're back with your husband and that he needs to keep it moving?"

"I did, but he won't. He says he's in love with me."

She let out a laugh. "Damn, you put it on his ass, didn't you? Let me find out you got skills."

I sipped my wine, swirling what was left in the glass as I allowed my mind to wander back to some of my more adventurous sexual escapades with Michael. Damn, we had had some good times together.

"We put it on each other. That's the problem."

Egypt got a troubled look on her face. "Oh my goodness. Are you still sleeping with him?"

"No, I swear." I raised my right hand. I didn't want her to

think less of me, and she probably would have left it alone, but then I slipped up. "I broke it off a few months ago, when Leon and I renewed our vows."

"But you've been back with Leon almost a year. . . . Hold up . . ." I could see her doing the math in her head, and then her mouth kind of fell open as she finished her calculations. "You were messing with them both at the same time?"

I lifted my glass and drained it in a feeble attempt to hide my face. This was humiliating. "Can I get a refill, please?"

"Damn, this Michael must be one special guy." She ignored the empty wineglass I'd placed back on the bar.

"If we'd gotten together before me and Leon, we'd be married right now."

"Oh my God. You're in love with this guy, aren't you? That's the real reason you're worried he's come back. You're in love with him!"

"I love my husband, Egypt," I said matter-of-factly, hoping my response didn't sound too automatic and hollow. I did not want her confusing the facts. Hell, I didn't want to confuse the facts. I did love Leon.

"Yeah, but you love Michael, too, don't you? That's why you asked me if I'd ever been in love with anyone other than Rashad right before you renewed your vows. You were thinking about Michael."

I gestured at my glass. "My wine? Can I get a refill on my wine?"

"Stop playing, Loraine. You're in love with two men, aren't you?"

"I love my husband, Egypt."

"Stop avoiding my question," she snapped. I reached for the bottle and she grabbed my wrist.

"I'm not avoiding your question. My answer is I love my husband. There is no answer other than that," I said adamantly, pulling my arm and the wine back to my side of the bar. "This wouldn't even be an issue if it wasn't for Leon's problem with sex."

"Leon has problems with sex? You never told me that." Now she was going to be laughing behind his back. Dammit, why did I have to go and open my big mouth? Coming here was a bad idea. I hated to say it, but I never had to censor my words around Jerome. I could say anything to him and not worry about having it come back to bite me. Would I ever find another friend like that?

"What type of problems?" Egypt asked, pushing for some juicy details I wasn't about to offer up.

"I'd rather not talk about that. It's not exactly something I want to go around jabbering about. And don't be judging him, please. Not being able to perform is a real blow to a man's ego."

"Who the hell am I to judge anybody? I'm the woman who can't have babies, remember? In a way, I can relate."

We were both quiet. Egypt's infertility was a tough subject for her, and I was surprised she'd even mentioned it. I let her process her thoughts for a moment, after which she brought the subject away from that difficult topic.

"Lots of men have problems in that area. Maybe he should talk to his doctor about Viagra or something. I heard those little blue pills work wonders."

"I wish a pill could solve his problem, but it's a lot deeper than that."

"What do you mean?"

Oh, how I wish she didn't feel the need to keep digging deeper. But at the same time, I hadn't been able to talk to anyone about how hard it was for me to deal with Leon's problem. I felt bad for him because he felt inadequate, but I couldn't deny that it was no picnic for me either. I was kind of curious how another woman would react. Would she think I was selfish?

I blurted out, "Leon has a problem with premature ejaculation."

"Oh, my . . . I'm sorry." I felt myself relax a little. I knew she meant she felt sorry for me, as a wife, having to deal with that. "I know that has to be difficult."

"*Difficult* isn't even the word. I mean, I love Leon, and I want to remain true to him, but this has been going on for five, almost six years. You know you hate to kick a dog when he's down, and when we took that vow, we said for better or worse. . . . I honestly meant it, but every once in a while, a girl needs . . . well, you know."

"Wow. Yeah, I do. I don't know what I'd do if I were in your shoes. I ain't gonna lie. I might go out there and find me some side dick too."

It felt good to laugh and relieve some of the tension that had been sitting on my shoulders. "It didn't always used to be this way. When we first got married, Leon was like a stallion that I wanted to ride all the time. Then after his uncle's death, things just went south. But I got used to it, until we separated and I met Michael."

She nodded like she knew exactly what I was saying.

"Egypt, he's woken up things I don't think I can live without, and now he's showing up at my door to remind me of them."

"I wouldn't beat myself up over this," she advised. I was starting to feel better about having shared this with her. It felt good to get some support for a change, instead of always playing the role of supportive wife. "Leon needs to step up, and if he's not up to the job, well, then maybe he should move over for a man who can."

Wait. Maybe she was taking this even a little further than was necessary.

"No, it's not like that. You've got to understand. I love Leon, and he's really working on his problem. He's seeing a doctor, trying to get help. I'm going to stick by him. I just don't need Michael constantly reminding me of what I'm not getting."

"No, you sure don't." Egypt reached over and hugged me like a true friend would. "A word of advice, Loraine: You keep this Michael as far away as you can, because a man like that has a way of seducing a woman's soul. Trust me, I know. That's what happened to me and Rashad, and I'm still trying to clean up the mess our relationship caused within my family." Although I appreciated Egypt's vote of encouragement, I wasn't too sure inside. How could I fight down the feelings that remained lodged in my heart for Michael?

Michael

10

Thank goodness I was the owner, because I didn't stroll into work until late in the afternoon. I'd actually been doing a lot of that lately. After seeing Loraine take Leon to what used to be *our* spot, I'd been throwing daily pity parties for myself. As I strolled through the gym, headed toward my office, I was prepared to do it again. My mind was on the bottle of tequila in the top drawer of my desk. I guess my mood was written all over my face, because Gordon, an old friend and the manager of the facility, furrowed his brow and said, "You look like you could use a drink."

"No, I could use two drinks," I replied.

"Well, before you get into a drunken stupor, we've got real problems." I looked at him with a frown, wishing he wouldn't continue. But of course he did. "We got two treadmills down, and Connie called in sick, so I'm gonna have to do the seven o'clock step class myself."

He didn't sound too happy about that, but I really didn't care. I had other things on my mind. "Okay, man. Teach the class." I walked past him and opened the door to my private office, hoping he would get the hint and leave me alone. All I really cared about was getting to that bottle.

"Mike, you listening to me, man?" Gordon got up and followed me into my office. He entered just as I was sitting down at my desk, before I had a chance to open the drawer and pull out the bottle. "We got problems. What do you want me to do?"

"I want you to handle it, dammit!" I snapped. "Isn't that what I pay you for? Do I have to micromanage everything around here?" He didn't deserve it, but I was taking out my frustration on him.

"Hey, look. I just wanted you to know. It's your money I'm planning on spending for new treadmills. If you don't give a shit, neither do I." He gave me attitude right back, and I was about to snap at him, but I caught myself.

"Look, G, I know you were trying to look out for me. I just have a lot on my mind." I pulled out the tequila and a glass and poured myself a shot. I would have pulled out two, but Gordon never drank until his shift was over—a discipline I used to prescribe to myself.

"Translation: You went to see Loraine again, and she sent your ass back here with your head between your legs."

"What are you, a fucking mind reader?" I threw back the shot and swallowed it, feeling the fire in the back of my throat.

"Sorry, Mike, but you don't have to be a mind reader to see she's just not into you like that anymore. The woman used to call here every day looking for you. She hasn't called in months."

I rolled my eyes. Why the hell couldn't anyone see what I was seeing?

"Sooner or later, you're going to have to face facts. You were just a little something-something while her husband was getting his act together."

I didn't acknowledge his point. Instead, I asked, "What's the definition of a stalker?"

Gordon narrowed his eyes at me as if he already knew exactly where I was going with this. "Someone who follows you around unwanted."

Jesus, maybe I was stalking her.

"Do you think I'm stalking Loraine?"

"No, I think you're trying to win her back, but she may not see it that way, and she's the only one who counts. There's a thin line between being in love and being obsessed."

"I'm not trying to stalk her. I just want her to talk to me. Is that so bad?"

"I don't know; you tell me. You've lost about fifteen pounds. You barely come to work, and when you're here, all you do is talk about Loraine this and Loraine that. If you're not obsessed, you're getting there, and that's not good."

I didn't bother to deny it. I guess I was acting crazy, but as far as I was concerned, my craziness was warranted. I needed Loraine to remember what we had together, and then she'd see she was really supposed to be with me.

I heaved a sigh. "G, I hear you loud and clear, but I just can't give up. We're meant to be."

"Hey, give it a rest. Women don't accuse men of stalking them if they're meant to be together. Now, I don't know what you're doing, but it's pretty obvious she ain't interested, and if you push it too far, you might end up in jail." I swear, nothing like a good friend to give it to you straight.

"So what do you think I should do?"

"I think you need to move on before you get yourself thrown in jail. That lady's got a lot of friends at city hall. It's time to move on, Mike."

I laughed. "She told me I need to move on too."

"Maybe you should take her advice."

"Maybe."

"Speaking of moving on, Celeste called three times."

"What does she want?" I sighed. Celeste Monroe was a former physical training client. She was really pretty, with a fantastic figure and a good head on her shoulders. To put it in a few words, she really had her shit together. I would have had to be blind not to see she was interested, and a fool not to be interested myself. I tried to keep it professional, so things never got off the ground between us. When she was at a point where she didn't need a coach anymore, I'd already started seeing Loraine, so it didn't matter how beautiful Celeste was; I wasn't interested.

Recently, Celeste had found out Loraine and I weren't together, and she had been trying to hook up on a date. Many of my friends, including Gordon, thought she was the one. Of course, I was preoccupied with getting Loraine back, but Celeste wouldn't take no for an answer.

"She wanted to speak to you." I guess Gordon read my look of dismissal, because he said, "I don't understand why you won't give her a chance, man."

"Hmph," I grunted.

"You know what? You're pathetic. Here you are running behind a married woman like some lovesick fool when you got a woman like Celeste worshipping the ground you walk on."

"I don't want a woman who worships the ground I walk on, G. I want Loraine."

"You haven't even given the woman a chance, Mike. Meanwhile, a guy like me can't get a girl like Celeste to give him the time of day. Man, I swear life just ain't fair."

"Man, if life was fair, I'd be with Loraine right now."

After two and a half weeks of feeling sorry for myself, no word from Loraine, and Gordon pushing me like he was my momma looking to have grandkids, I finally relented and went out with Celeste a few times. I'd be lying if I didn't admit I had a good time. She was a special woman who kept me laughing and intrigued whenever we were together; but despite all that, I still thought of Loraine constantly. I just couldn't get her out of my head. I woke up thinking about her and went to sleep with an image of her in my mind. I was whipped with a capital *W*.

I wasn't trying to be two-faced with Celeste. From day one, I was straight up with her about my feelings for Loraine. I told her I was still deeply in love with my ex, and if by chance she'd take me back, I'd drop everything to be with her. Surprisingly, Celeste didn't seem to care. From what she said, she just wanted time to show me what kind of woman she was and could be to me. After that, let the chips fall where they may. I liked her attitude but wondered when it came down to it if she would really practice what she preached.

Either way, I decided to take it slow. We were on our fourth date before I invited her to my house. All we did was watch TV. I was a big fan of *Heroes,* and as it turned out, so was Celeste. I made my special salad with grilled chicken, walnuts, and dried cranberries, which Celeste loved, and we sat in front of the TV, enjoying dinner and a glass of wine while we watched the show.

When it was over, I left Celeste in the living room and took the dirty dishes into the kitchen. When I returned, she was standing in front of my mantel, holding a framed picture of Loraine and me. Gordon had told me about ten times to get rid of that picture, or at least remove it from plain sight. I'd taken down all the photos in my office, but I never did move this one. It was my favorite picture of us from when we went to Martha's Vineyard during the time she and Leon were separated. We were all hugged up and smiling big, bright smiles into the camera. Anyone who saw that picture could tell how much in love we were.

"Is this your ex?"

"Yeah, that's her." I nodded a little apprehensively. I got up and took the picture out of her hand, placing it back on the mantel. I expected Celeste to comment about her looks, or maybe her size, but she didn't.

"You look happy," was all Celeste said as she walked back over to the sofa and sat down.

"We were happy. I hope it doesn't bother you that I still have that picture up, but I'm not moving it right now."

Celeste let out a sigh. "I can't say that it doesn't bother me, because I'd be telling a lie. I just don't want any surprises or to be disrespected. If you and this woman get back together, I just want you to tell me. I don't want to hear it from anyone else."

"That's only fair." I sat down next to her and took her hand. "I promise if it happens, you won't hear it from anyone but me."

The next thing I knew, Celeste kissed me on the mouth. At first, it was a slow, tentative kiss; then it became a little more passionate. Ten minutes later, we were still fully clothed, but I was lying on top of her. My hands were roaming her body freely, while hers struggled to loosen my belt.

We were both intoxicated with lust until she said, "Michael, condom's in my purse, but I can't reach it."

Suddenly, I was alert. I was sober. Everything I was doing was real, and real meant consequences.

From where I lay, I looked up and saw the picture of Loraine. I pulled away from Celeste. "I can't do this, Celeste."

"Why? What did I do?"

"You didn't do anything. I'm just not ready for this. Not yet anyway."

Celeste smiled and gave me a gentle, understanding kiss. "Take your time. I'm not going anywhere."

Jerome

11

"Hey, Jerome, I just wanted to apologize."

I was at the Waffle House in Danville, drinking a cup of coffee and admiring Ron's flawless skin, when he put down his fork to address me. He'd just devoured a twelve-ounce steak, three scrambled eggs, hash browns, and six slices of toast in mere minutes. I had an appetite like that, too, when I was younger, but with age came the understanding that if I ate like that now, I'd be twice my size.

Ron had loosened up a little since we left the police station, and I was starting to see glimpses of the old happy-go-lucky Ron, but there was no doubt the past year had taken quite a toll on him. I had convinced him to stay at a hotel near my place in Richmond for the weekend, once we got his car out of impound. My next objective was to convince him that he needed to share that room with me.

"What exactly are you apologizing for?"

"I don't know. Everything, I guess. I'm not exactly proud of the way things went down last time I saw you. You've been nothing but nice to me. I just freaked out. I wasn't ready for that kind of exposure. I'm still not."

"Hey, I understand. I wish you could have walked out of the closet instead of being thrown out of it. I never wanted that for you."

"I wish that day never happened."

Although the whole incident was Peter's fault, the two of us were the ones feeling shitty about it. What was the point of that?

If we let it keep us down, then Peter had won. I tried to change the subject. "Hey, man. Are you working?"

He frowned. "I was working over at the movie theater, but I doubt I got a job now."

"Why's that?"

"The guy I assaulted was my manager."

"What'd he do? Cheat you out of some hours?" If that were the case, beating the guy up was a pretty extreme reaction, but I was sure Ron was carrying around a lot of pent-up anger ever since he'd had to drop out of school in disgrace.

"No, it wasn't over hours. It's complicated."

Now I was intrigued. Was it possible it was a lover's quarrel gone into overdrive? I wouldn't have expected Ron to be dating any guys, at least not yet. The night he punched me in the face and told me he didn't want to see me anymore, I assumed he would leave the gay lifestyle alone, at least until he sorted out everything. If he was dating men, I definitely wanted to know about it, because it might improve my chances of getting back into bed with him.

"I consider myself a bright guy, and I don't have nowhere to be, so spill it," I said.

"Let's put it this way: Danville's not like Richmond. It's a small town. Everybody knows me down here. I used to be a big star. When I came home, they all wanted to know why I wasn't in school."

I grimaced, because I could imagine how difficult that must have been for a kid who was far from ready to be out and proud. "What'd you tell them?"

"I just told them that school wasn't for me. Most of them probably thought I was a Prop Eight student, anyway, so they left me alone. But then word started getting around about the pictures and me being gay. I know people were talking behind my back, because it was driving my mom crazy.

"I was dealing with it the best I could, trying to ignore it, but two days ago, my manager, this flaming dude, comes up to me, right in my face, and asks me if I'm sweet. I'm sorry, but I tried to break his freaking jaw."

I shook my head. I'd run into a few guys like this in my life, gay men who flounce around like women and expect every other gay man to be down with it. They have no idea how hard they make it for those of us who happen to love men but aren't trying to throw it in everyone's faces. "Well, you're right; you can't go back to that job. But if I was there, I would have beat the crap out of that guy myself."

He smiled for the first time.

"So what do you want to do with yourself?"

"I'd love to go back to school, but all I ever wanted to do was play ball. I'd give anything to be back out on that court. I guess that's the real reason I was so mad at you for so long. I used to think that if I hadn't met you, I'd still be in school playing ball."

"And for that, I'm sorry, Ron. I wasn't trying to—"

"Hold up." He reached across the table and touched my hand lightly. "I'm not trying to blame this on you anymore. You didn't force me into anything. All you did was open a door. I was the one who walked through it; but I'm no sissy, Jerome. I'm a man."

"I know that. No one knows that better than me."

"But society doesn't. Society thinks we're monsters—and so does my momma." The words rushed from his mouth, and my heart ached for him. I don't care who you like to sleep with; no one should have to feel rejection from his own mother.

I reasoned, "Society's changing, and well, no disrespect, but your momma is just plain wrong."

"Don't I know it. We live in the same house, and she barely speaks to me. I know she's embarrassed, but I never thought my momma would turn her back on me. I just feel like running away somewhere where nobody knows me."

"I feel you on that one." I'd had the same fantasy during times of trouble. In fact, a few times I'd gotten on a plane and escaped for a while to get my head on straight, though I always returned home to Virginia. "You ever been to Europe?"

"Nope. Always wanted to go to Paris, though."

"Paris is nice. People are a lot more tolerant over there. Good place to start over. You'd like it."

"You act like I should go there or something."

"You should."

He shot me a dismissive glance. "On what, my looks? I'm un-employed and owe you for bailing me out. I ain't got no money to be moving to France."

"You know, if you put your mind to it, you could make it on your looks—but I'm betting on your jump shot."

"There's no way I can go back to the game now that everyone knows about me. No one wants to be in the locker room with a gay guy. It's like they think I'm not there to play the game but to stare at their ugly asses in the shower."

"I'm not talking about playing ball here."

"Then what are you talking about?"

"I'm talking about you playing ball for a European pro team."

"And how the hell am I supposed to do that? It's not like I'm playing somewhere now where scouts can come check me out."

He was taking the pessimistic viewpoint, but the more I talked about this idea, the more I believed it really could work.

"You know," I told him, "there are some advantages to being gay. We got one hell of a network, and a lot of resources."

"Like what?" he asked, obviously still doubtful.

"I know some people who can get you on in Europe. They have plenty of openly gay players over there." Then I took a leap of faith and suggested something I almost didn't realize I'd been thinking before I said it. "We can both move there. I mean, if that sounds all right to you."

He stared at me for a long, uncomfortable minute before he spoke. I hoped he was seriously considering my plan, but if he was, he still needed more convincing. "Just pack up and move to Europe. Are you crazy? We can't do that."

"Why not? I don't have anything holding me to this place. I work for myself as a consultant, and I could do most of that over the Internet and by fax. I could lease my house. I have only one thing and that's . . . really nothing." I meant it too. Things were really iffy between Big Poppa and me. After all this time waiting for him to leave his wife and love me completely, I was beginning to realize it was something that might never happen. Going to Europe with Ron would be a chance for me to finally live my life on my terms.

"Really, you'd give up your life here?"

"Why not? Things aren't going that well for me here. I'd like a fresh start, too, as long as it's with you."

"Jerome, you better not be playing with me." For the first time that day, I saw a glimmer of hope in his eyes.

"Look, everything is going to be all right—that is, if you want it to be all right."

Ron leaned back and released a genuine laugh. "You know, I really missed you."

"I missed you too. So, what do you think? Is it a plan?"

Ron didn't answer. He just got out of his seat and picked up his coat. "Let's get out of here."

I left a twenty-dollar bill on the table, and we headed for the exit. As we stepped into the parking lot, I took a chance and reached for Ron's hand. He didn't exactly grab mine eagerly, but he didn't push me away either.

"You okay with this?" I asked.

He stopped walking and turned to me. "I don't know yet. It doesn't feel comfortable, but I gotta start somewhere, right?"

"Right," I said hopefully.

"Just let me take it slow, okay? I'm still not sure I want to go advertising this to the world yet."

"No problem." I released his hand and patted his shoulder to let him know I meant it. After everything he'd suffered through, I wasn't about to place any unreasonable demands on him. I would allow him to grow comfortable with his sexuality at his own pace. Unfortunately, someone else had other plans.

"Aw, isn't that cute. Jerome's back with his little boy toy Ron. Hey, Ron, you didn't drop the soap while you were locked up, did you?" He laughed like a hyena.

Every muscle in my body tensed up. How the hell had Peter found us here? As fast as I had been driving to get to the jail earlier, there's no way he could have followed me. I didn't realize it at the time, but now I believe he had been keeping an eye on Ron—and who knows how many other former lovers—on the off chance he needed blackmail material to prevent me from getting back together with any of them. He had somehow learned about the arrest, and for all I knew, he'd been at the jail before I even got there. Don't ask me how this psycho managed to have a real job with all the time he seemed to spend destroying my love life.

I saw a camera flash as Peter announced, "Hold still. This will look great on the cover of the *Danville Register and Bee*."

"Who the hell is that?" Ron asked.

"That's the son of a bitch who sent our picture to your family and friends last—" I didn't even finish my sentence before Ron was on top of Peter.

"You're the motherfucker who ruined my life! I'm gonna kill you," Ron screamed repeatedly as he threw blow after blow.

Peter was hell with a camera, but he was no match for Ron's athletic performance. He fell to the ground and covered his head. Ron stopped delivering punches, but he wasn't finished with Peter quite yet. He spotted the camera lying beside Peter and raised it high in the air.

"Stop it, Ron! Stop! He ain't worth it," I shouted, terrified that I was about to witness Peter's brains being splattered all over the pavement. Not that I wouldn't have enjoyed having Peter out of my life, but Ron would have suffered serious consequences. The judge sure as hell wouldn't have given him no thousand-dollar bail for a murder charge.

It took all my strength to pull Ron off of Peter. "Come on, man. You just got out of jail. He's not worth it. Let's get out of here."

Ron finally came to his senses and lowered the camera to his side. He took one last look at Peter, who was still cowering in the fetal position on the ground, and then Ron spit on him. He threw the camera against the concrete, stomping on it a few times for good measure, until it lay in pieces.

I took his arm and gently led him away toward my car.

Peter wiped blood from his mouth and gathered enough strength to call out, "This isn't over, Jerome. Not by a long shot! I swear to God I'm gonna get you both if it's the last thing I do!"

Leon

12

I opened my eyes to the pleasant sight of two large breasts hovering over me. I loved Loraine's tits and she knew it. They swung, smacking me playfully in the face, and every once in a while, a nipple would slide in front of my hungry lips. I would suck it until the other breast knocked it away. She lowered her chest until my head was the center of a tittie sandwich, which made me laugh. I kissed between her breasts as she squeezed them on either side of my head. I always loved it when Loraine was playful, but after a while, it was becoming uncomfortable.

I lifted my arms to ease her off me, because I was having trouble breathing, but my arms wouldn't budge, and that's when I realized they were tied down.

"Baby, please, I can't breathe," I managed to say between short breaths, but the more I struggled, the more weight she placed on me. Was she trying to kill me? Why wouldn't she get up? I struggled for air, but like I said, the more I struggled, the more weight she applied. I thought about trying to twist my way out, but like my arms, I was horrified to find my legs were tied down too. Jesus Christ, my wife was trying to kill me, and it looked like she was going to succeed!

Finally, she took pity on me and sat up. Unfortunately, that was only the beginning of my horror, because when I saw her face, I felt like I was going to pass out. It wasn't my beloved Loraine who was trying to kill me; it was Aunt Barbara, and she wasn't showing me any real pity. She was just repositioning her triple-D breasts to make it easier to suffocate me.

"Now you'll be with me forever, baby," she said.

As she lowered her breasts down on my face again, I was helpless to do anything except scream, so that was what I did.

"Aunt Barbara, please, please! I don't want to die!"

"Leon, Leon, honey, wake up! You're dreaming again."

Loraine was shaking me when I opened my eyes this time. I can't begin to tell you how relieved I was to see her face. "You okay?"

I nodded. "Yeah, I'm okay. God, it was so real."

"Was your uncle beating you with a damn strap again?"

"No, no, it was my aunt." I sat up and wiped my forehead, noticing that the sheets were damp because I had been sweating so profusely.

"Your aunt was beating you?"

"She was trying to kill me, Loraine," I said, still trying to make sense of the dream. "My aunt Barbara was trying to kill me." I wasn't about to tell her how.

From her expression, it was clear that this news confused Loraine. I'd never had a negative thing to say about Aunt Barbara. While my nightmares about my abusive uncle made sense to her, she had no information to help her understand why I would be having bad dreams about my beloved aunt. "Why would she want to kill you? She loved you, didn't she?"

"Yeah, she loved me all right."

Loraine picked up on my sarcasm right away. "I thought it was your uncle who beat you. Are you trying to say your aunt was in on it too?"

I didn't answer her. Instead, I got up and walked into the bathroom. I guess I was hoping that would be enough to make her drop the subject, but it wasn't. She followed me, pestering me with more questions as I urinated. It had been two weeks since the hypnosis session that uncovered the memories about my first kiss. Since then, I'd been hypnotized two more times and had recalled quite a bit more about my past that had been buried deep in my subconscious. Most of it was very embarrassing, but at least I was starting to get some answers about who and what I really was. I hadn't shared any of this with Loraine, because I was afraid that the disturbing truths about my past—and the man I had become because of it—might be more than she could handle. It might be the last straw that would finally break up our marriage.

"Are you ever going to talk to me about what happened when the doctor hypnotized you? I'm not stupid, you know. I know you found out more about your aunt and uncle than you're saying." Loraine's voice was stern. "How can I help you if I don't know what is going on?"

As I moved from the toilet to the sink to wash my hands, I held her stare. She kept looking at me, her eyes commanding me to speak about what was in my heart. She wouldn't break the stare. She waited patiently until I finished washing my hands, and then she blocked my exit from the bathroom.

"Honey, can you please move out of the way?" I lifted my hands up, showing my palms in a noncombative gesture.

"Sure, if you promise to tell me what the hell is going on. The doctor has hypnotized you three times in the past two weeks, and you haven't told me a thing. I have a fucking right to know, Leon. I'm your wife!"

"Sweetheart, be careful what you ask for. I've recently learned that there are some doors you don't want to open."

"I'm a big girl. I can handle it. I took you for better or for worse, remember?"

That kind of pushed a button for me. Where was that commitment to "for better or for worse" when she thought I was cheating and she kicked me out of the house? To tell you the truth, sometimes it felt like I was the one doing all the work to keep us together. She had allowed herself to be duped by Jerome when he framed me as a cheater, yet I was the one going through this difficult therapy, as if my sexual performance was the only problem we had. What about her problem with trust, which we never really addressed after she asked me to come back home? She apologized to me, but she never considered the idea that maybe she had some issues of her own that caused her to be so distrustful. Well, fine. If she was such a big girl now and wanted to see what "for worse" really meant, then I would tell her what hypnosis had uncovered.

"Okay, Big Sexy, if you wanna know, I'll tell you. I just hope you don't go running for the hills once you know the truth."

This caused her to look a little apprehensive, but I knew Loraine, and she was not one to back down easily. She stepped out of the way to let me out of the bathroom. "I want to know, Leon. You can tell me, whatever it is."

I walked past her and sat on the bed. She took a seat next to me and placed her hand over mine.

I took a deep breath and admitted to her what I'd learned in my first hypnosis session about kissing my aunt. Loraine didn't say a word; she just squeezed my hand. Only time would tell if she'd still be so supportive after I explained what I'd learned in sessions two and three.

"The next time the doctor hypnotized me, I went back to a time around a year after that first kiss."

She flinched almost imperceptibly, probably because I'd referred to it as the first kiss.

I nodded in answer to her silent question. "Yeah, it was the first, but definitely not the last kiss." By now, I was feeling some strange relief in spilling my guts to her, so I continued without any prompting on her part. "But in this second session, I realized that my aunt seduced me into having sex with her on a regular basis to keep me around."

Loraine's hand flew to her mouth. "Oh my God. I can't believe she did that to you. You were just a kid."

"I was fourteen," I corrected, though I wasn't sure why. It was almost like I was defending Aunt Barbara, like sex with a fourteen-year-old nephew was any less offensive than one who was younger. I would have to talk to Roberta about why I did that.

Loraine looked like she was sick to her stomach.

"I know; it's disgusting," I said. I waited for her to speak, but it looked like she was having trouble even processing the information. Part of me was relieved she hadn't run from the room screaming at this point, but it was driving me crazy that she didn't speak. Was she judging me? I felt the need to defend myself from her silence. "How do you think I feel? Loraine, I can't even imagine myself doing that, and now I've got these images instilled in my brain. Roberta says I blocked all this from my conscious mind until now because I was trying to protect myself. I can see what she means, because some days I feel like it's enough to drive me crazy."

"You never told anyone this was happening?" she asked, and sadly, it sounded like there was judgment in her question.

"I was a kid. I was confused. Roberta says it's not uncommon for a child, even a teenager, to do nothing to stop it. After all, this was a woman who loved me. She took care of me when I had no one else who would. It's hard for a kid to truly understand that someone who loves you so much can also hurt you, can do bad things. Now I'm starting to understand that what she did changed the man I became. Even now, I have a hard time understanding the difference between right and wrong, because Aunt Barbara was so good to me and so bad at the same time."

"But maybe if you had told someone—"

I put up my hand to stop her. "It's okay, Loraine. I don't expect you to understand. That's why I didn't want to tell you in the first place. But you can tell me the truth. You think I'm some kind of freak now, don't you?"

Loraine waited before she spoke, as if she wanted to pick her words carefully. "Baby, it's not your fault. You were just a child doing what you were told. Your aunt was sick, and so was your uncle."

"So anyway . . . ," I started, trying to sound lighthearted as I redirected the conversation. "Roberta thinks this stuff with my aunt is the key to this whole premature ejaculation thing." I would have to live with these memories every day now that they'd resurfaced, and so would Loraine now that I'd revealed them to her. At least we could try to focus on the good that might come out of it.

"She does?" Loraine's whole demeanor changed.

"Yeah, seems my aunt was so afraid we'd get caught by my uncle that she would rush me to ejaculations. Somehow, she trained my body to conform to what she wanted. Dr. Marshall feels likes it's just a matter of time before she finds the switch in my mind that will snap me back to normal."

Loraine heaved a sigh of relief, and I swear I could see every muscle in her body relax. "I'm not gonna lie, honey. I'm just glad to know it's not me. For a while, I thought it was my fault."

"Oh, no, baby. It was never your fault. I find you to be one of the sexiest women alive. It's just I'm all messed up inside. I've got to work this stuff through." I reached for her hand. "Do you hate me for what happened?"

"Leon, how could you say that? The wrong was done to you. You were a minor." This time, I didn't doubt her sincerity. She wasn't just feeding me words to prove she was on my side. She was truly accepting me and all the baggage I'd just brought into our already-challenging relationship.

Loraine tilted up my chin and kissed me tenderly. "We can get through this together."

I felt tears of appreciation flood my eyes. "Loraine, I love you. You're the best. Thank you for being here for me."

As she held me in her arms, just the feeling of her big breasts against my chest had me aroused. I gave her a deep kiss and tried to fondle her, but it wasn't long before she gently eased herself out of my reach.

"How about if we don't have sex while you work this through. That way you won't have that added pressure on you."

Loraine had hit the nail on the head; sex usually did end up making me feel pressured. If I could work through my feelings about me and my aunt, it might fix that problem in the long run, but I never would have dreamed of suggesting no sex to my wife. I was way too afraid she'd leave me. I had to make sure that she was really okay with it now.

"You think that's a good idea?"

"Yeah. We can just cuddle and hug. Sex isn't that important if two people love each other, Leon." Loraine climbed back into bed and held out her arms.

I happily nestled up next to her and got cozy in Loraine's soft embrace, where I slept peacefully for the first time in a long time.

Michael

13

"I cannot wait to get you home tonight," Celeste purred on the dance floor, our bodies intertwining as if we were one. We'd been flirting back and forth since the moment we'd arrived at the Annual African American Dance for Literacy at the Marriott hotel on Broad Street. So far, it had been a night to remember. The food was excellent, they had a great band with a Beyoncé clone, whose singing could have passed for the real thing, and, more importantly, they were giving away five $10,000 college scholarships.

"I just hope you know what to do with me when you get me there," I teased.

"Well, if I don't, I'll make it up as I go. So be prepared for anything—and I mean anything." She turned around and ground her plump, round hips into my groin.

For the next song, the band slowed things down, and Celeste wrapped her arms around my neck, while mine slid around her waist. All in all, as dates go, I'd give this one an eight out of ten, with a definite possibility for improvement as the night went on. We'd been dating for almost a month, and Celeste had made it clear that it was time for us to seal the deal. From the way my manhood was reacting to her bumping and grinding on the dance floor, I was apt to agree with her. It had been four months since I'd been with Loraine—a long, hard four months, and I had to admit I was about due. Nothing short of a miracle was going to keep me and Celeste from consummating our relationship tonight.

"Aw, hell fucking no. You have got to be kidding me," Celeste cursed.

"Sorry." I immediately lifted my hands, which I had slid down from her waist to her hips and ass. I didn't really think she was going to have a problem with it after the way we'd been dancing, but that'll tell you how much I know about women.

"No, that's not it." She guided my hands back down over her ass.

I wasn't about to argue with her, but I was curious about why she'd cursed. "Everything all right?"

"I don't know; you tell me. Isn't that your ex over there?"

"Where?" I didn't mean to seem so eager, but my neck did snap around on its axis as I spun her around. "I don't see her."

"By that pole, staring at us."

I looked in the direction that Celeste was gazing, and I saw Loraine, along with that chump husband of hers. He hadn't seen me, but Loraine's eyes were fixated on us like laser beams. Once again, I lifted my hands from Celeste's ass. I could feel her body stiffen, which told me she wasn't very happy about it.

What was Loraine doing here? Then again, why wouldn't she be here? She was damn near the mayor of Richmond with all the people she knew.

I must have been gawking a little too long because Celeste pinched my arm. "I think it's time we leave."

I took another look at Loraine and sighed. "You know what? I think you're right." Best for me to get my behind outta there. I could feel in my bones that sticking around was going to be nothing but trouble. Maybe if I took Celeste home and she put it on me like she'd been promising all night, I'd be able to erase from my mind the image of Loraine and her death stare.

The second her arms came from around my neck, Celeste took my arm and practically marched me off the dance floor. There was no doubt in my mind she was sending Loraine a very clear message: *He's mine, bitch!*

As we headed for the coat check, I couldn't help but sneak another peek at Loraine. She had a sour expression on her face, but she still looked damn good.

I handed Celeste our coat claims. "I'll be right back. I have to go to the restroom."

It wasn't that I was planning on going to talk to Loraine. In fact, I really didn't know what I wanted to do. But I did know that this silent tug-of-war between the two women had me feeling claustrophobic. My escape to the men's room was just an excuse to put some physical distance between me and this situation.

Celeste wasn't about to let me get away that easy. She tightened her grip on my hand. "You okay? Are you still spending the night at my house?"

"Ain't nothing changed, Celeste." I took her in my arms and gave her a reassuring kiss.

"Good. Now, hurry back—and make sure you wash your hands." She slapped me on the butt playfully as I walked away.

Fortunately, I didn't have to pass by Loraine on my way to the bathroom. I figured I could spend a few minutes in there gathering my thoughts, and then Celeste and I could get out of there. At least that's the way I thought it would go down. But Loraine had other ideas, as she was standing outside the men's room with her arms folded and a scowl on her face when I exited.

"Loraine . . ." For a brief second, it crossed my mind that maybe she was just standing there waiting for Leon to come out of the men's room, but the look on her face made me dismiss that thought quickly. Her angry glare was directed right at me. I tried to avoid looking into her eyes, but that only made me notice the purple dress she was wearing. It was one I'd seen before, and I loved the way it showed off her thick shape. A rush of emotions overcame me all at once. I was happy to see her. I was physically aroused by the sight of her. I wanted to hear her say she was wrong to leave me and that she loved me as much as I loved her. But in spite of all those feelings, I couldn't ignore the way she was glowering and the harsh words she spoke.

"Don't Loraine me! Who the hell was that?"

"Who was what? What are you talking about?"

She pointed a finger in my face. "Don't play stupid with me, Michael. Who the hell was that trashy-ass woman you were feeling all over?"

"You mean Celeste? Celeste isn't trashy." I suppressed a smirk. It gave me a certain sense of satisfaction to know that the sight of me with another woman made Loraine jealous. It was the least she deserved after all the pain she'd put me through. Yeah, I loved Loraine, but that didn't mean she didn't deserve a little bit of payback.

"Michael, you wouldn't know trashy if it hit you in the face. If you don't have respect for yourself, at least have some for me. I can't believe you would bring some tramp up in my face like this."

Was she for real? "I didn't bring anyone in your face. I didn't even know you were coming here."

She laughed. "You are such a pathetic liar. You followed me all the way to Williamsburg; of course you would follow me to the club. You brought that woman here on purpose, trying to make me jealous."

I crossed my arms and leaned against the wall, raising my eyebrows in a look that suggested, *It worked, didn't it?* but Loraine wasn't about to admit defeat.

"Well, news flash: If you're trying to make me jealous, at least make sure it's an upgrade, because she's not even in my class. I can't believe you'd date someone so ugly."

"Don't talk about her like that. Celeste is not ugly by a long shot, and you know it. What is going on with you anyway? You didn't used to be so petty."

This stopped her for a second. Loraine prided herself on being classy, and her behavior was anything but that right now. I guess she realized it, as she took a deep breath and then tried to change directions. "Well, if she's so damn pretty, you need to be with her and leave me the hell alone."

Wow. She was jealous; there was no doubt about it. The way she had dismissed me in Williamsburg, I thought for sure she was done with me, but now she was practically begging me not to forget her. I guess seeing me with another woman reminded her of what I had to offer. Well, I had the upper hand now, and I wasn't ready to give it up yet.

"I am with her. And as far as leaving you alone, I don't know what you're talking about. It's been a long time since you've heard from me."

"Oh, please," she scoffed. "It wasn't that long ago you were circling my block with your lights turned off."

Okay, she got me with that one. I had done that a few times since the incident in Williamsburg, but I didn't know she'd seen me. Maybe it was time to end this battle of wills while I was still ahead. Let Loraine stew in her jealousy for a while.

"Look, Loraine, you're the one who dumped me and told me to move on, so that's what I'm trying to do. If I were you, I'd get used to seeing me and Celeste on the social scene."

She countered with, "You know what, Michael? You need to just get over me."

I was about to tell Loraine that it was the other way around when I heard Celeste's voice.

"Michael?" She stood a few feet away from us, holding our coats. She gave me a brilliant smile that I'm sure was more for Loraine's benefit. "Ready to go home, honey?"

I had to give her credit. She could have come tearing down the hall and gotten up in Loraine's face. You know, the typical "Back up off my man!" routine. But with just one smile, she'd let Loraine know that she had no doubt which one of them would be leaving with me. The funny thing was that she was totally right. As much as I wanted Loraine, as many times as I'd begged her to give things another chance, I didn't want her at this moment. She'd told me to move on, and dammit, I was going to prove that I could do just that.

"I'll be right there," I told Celeste, then turned back to Loraine. "I have to go. My date's calling me. But it was nice seeing you again, Loraine."

"Whatever," she huffed.

I took a few steps down the hall, then turned around and told her, "By the way, I always thought you looked hot in that purple dress."

Jerome

14

I'd just thrown some clean clothes in a bag and was on my way out the door, heading back to the Ramada Inn in Petersburg, where Ron was waiting for me. We'd been shacked up there for a couple of weeks, getting reacquainted intimately as we made plans for the future. Fortunately, there seemed to be no repercussions after the fight in the parking lot with Peter: no crazy phone calls, no knock at the door, and, most importantly, no cops looking to arrest Ron for assault. Still, to be safe, Ron pretty much stayed inside our room, and I rarely went out other than to pick up our takeout orders.

I was having the time of my life, and I was really feeling Ron. I know I've mentioned this before, but he made me feel young again. The more time I spent with him, the more I could really imagine us making a life together in Europe. There was just one obstacle—and it was standing in front of me now in the form of Big Poppa. Talk about bad timing. I would much rather have had this conversation over the phone.

"Where the hell have you been? I've been calling you day and night for two weeks, and you haven't returned one call." He was talking loud, but he looked more hurt than angry. It took me by surprise, because he was usually the one acting nonchalant, and I was the one wanting more.

"I've been busy," I replied, quickly zipping up my bag. I needed to get the hell out of there. Last thing I wanted was for him to start playing on my conscience.

"Too busy for me?" He spoke as if I'd insulted him.

"Yes, too busy for you."

His mouth hung open for a second, and he looked confused. I can't say that I blamed him. We'd had our share of spats over the years, but I'd always been the one eager to make up. But not this time; this time I wanted a clean break so I could give an honest effort to pursuing a relationship with Ron.

"Jerome, what's going on? What did I do?"

He sounded truly hurt, and I could feel my defenses weaken. It was definitely time to go. I tried to walk past him to leave the bedroom, but he blocked my way. His right hand slid around my waist. I took a step back, but it was too late. I'd gotten a whiff of his Polo cologne—yeah, it's old school, but so am I—and suddenly my heart softened. I tried to offer some explanation, in hopes that we could end this painlessly.

"It's not what you did; it's what you won't do. It's what you didn't do." My eyes traveled to his wedding ring to complete my point.

"This is about my wife? You still want me to leave her?" He was clearly annoyed. "You know I can't do that."

"That's because your marriage is the most important thing in your life." I tried to avoid his eyes, because they had always been my weakness. He tried to touch my face, but I turned my head to avoid it. "You know from my actions that I wanted to be the most important thing in your life. But that's just not possible, is it?"

"Look, Jerome, be fair," he begged. "You knew I was married when we started this thing. How often do I complain about these guys you be seeing?"

"Only reason you don't complain is because you didn't want me throwing your marriage in your face. You know what they say about people in glass houses." I tried to push my way past again, but he stood his ground.

I sighed. "Look, I still care about you, but it's better we end things now."

"End things?" His eyebrows shot up in shock. I bet he'd never expected me to be the one to end it. He shook his head vehemently. "Uh-uh. It's not over yet. You can't just walk out on me. I love your black ass."

"You don't love me. You love what I do for you. Love is a commitment."

"We are committed," he said. "Shit, we've been together for five years."

"No, we're not committed." I softened my tone. "And for a while, I was okay with that."

"But you're not now? What exactly are you saying, Jerome?"

"I'm trying to say it was nice while it lasted, but I've found someone. Someone who makes me happy. Someone I can grow old with."

"What do you mean you found someone? Didn't you hear me a little while ago? I said I love you." He exploded, pushing me backward against the wall and grabbing my shirt with both hands. I could have resisted, but at this point, he was his own worst enemy.

"If you love me, leave your wife." I pointed at the portable house phone on my dresser. "Call her. Tell her you're leaving her. You don't even have to tell her you're leaving her for a man. Just tell her you're leaving."

He looked at the phone but didn't move toward it.

"Come on," I challenged. "I wanna hear this."

He looked at the phone again and then back at me, but I knew he'd never make that call. I was issuing an ultimatum that I knew he could never live up to.

He let go of my shirt and turned away from me. "Who is he? Who's this guy you're going to be with?"

"You don't know him. He's someone from my past. We just reconnected."

"Is he better-looking than me?"

Oh, God, I'd never heard Big Poppa sound so pathetic.

"You're both good-looking men. But this isn't about vanity. This is about me being happy."

I took a step into the hallway, but he grabbed my arm to stop me.

"Don't do this, Jerome. I really do love you."

"If you really love me, be happy for me." I gave him a smile, but he looked like he was going to cry.

"I can't. I can't be happy for you if you're with some other dude." He stepped out of the way.

"Okay, then I've got to go."

I leaned over and kissed him on the cheek.

"How about one for the road?" he asked. I know he thought he sounded seductive, but all I heard was desperation.

"No, I don't think that's such a good idea. I'm in a relationship now. I'm saving all this good stuff for him."

"What he don't know won't hurt him."

"You need to give it up, because it's not happening."

"I can't believe this."

"Believe it," I told him as I picked up my bag and headed for the door.

He followed me outside, but thankfully he was done talking. I was too exhausted to deal with him anymore, not to mention the fact that Ron was probably wondering where the hell I was. My phone had been vibrating in my pocket the whole time I was trying to get rid of Big Poppa.

I pulled out the phone and saw that there had been several missed calls, all from Ron's number. I tried to call him back, but it went straight to his voice mail. He was probably trying to punish me for not picking up my phone before. It was all right, though, because I knew Ron would let me make it up to him later in the way I knew best.

I left him a message. "Hey, Ron. Sorry about not answering before. I had something to handle over here, but don't worry about it. Everything's taken care of, and I'll be on my way back soon. I'm just gonna stop and get something for us to eat. Maybe Mexican food . . . and, of course, you know what I'm bringing for dessert." I got in my car, looking forward to another hot night with my fine young man.

Michael

15

"You still coming in?" Celeste turned to me with questioning eyes.

We'd held hands the entire ride home, but neither of us said a word until we pulled into her driveway. I was pretty sure she was pissed off about seeing me talking to Loraine outside the men's room. I could only imagine how she might have interpreted what she saw. As for me, I was quiet because I was still trying to figure out what the hell had just happened. Don't get me wrong; it felt good to know that Loraine was jealous, but you couldn't have paid me to think she would be bold enough to camp out in front of the men's room at a major function just to confront me, especially with Leon in the building.

"Celeste, I'm sorry about what happened with Loraine. I wasn't trying to embarrass you. She followed me to the bathroom."

Celeste leaned in, and I braced myself for a smack, but instead she kissed me. "Thank you."

"Thank you?" I sat silently for a second. "So you're not mad at me?"

"For what? I heard you defending my honor. You were really sweet. I know that must have been tough." She kissed me again, then reached for the car door. "You coming in?"

"Yeah, I'm coming." Maybe this wasn't going to end up a bad night after all.

When we were inside, she placed her bag on the small table next to the door and threw her arms around my neck. She kissed me softly, smiling when our lips parted, then kissed me again passionately.

"I've been waiting to get you here all night."

"Well, you don't have to wait any longer. I'm here." I kissed her neck, and my hands roamed her backside, sliding under her dress until I felt the bare skin of each cheek. I had no idea who invented G-strings and thongs, but one day I'd love to buy him a drink. She arched her back, letting out a small moan when my finger massaged the thin material covering her clit.

"Oh! My, my, my, somebody knows what he's doing." She gently removed my hand from between her legs. "But I think we're getting a little ahead of ourselves. I've got a lot of plans for us tonight. So why don't we slow things down a bit."

I was reluctant to stop what we'd started, and only did so because she seemed to be offering the promise of bigger and better things to come.

"Why don't you fix us a drink?" she asked, leading me toward the small bar in her living room.

"Sure. What you drinking?"

"I don't know. Surprise me."

"Okay." She had everything necessary to make apple martinis, so I got to work.

She came up behind me and gave me a kiss on the neck that sent shivers up my spine. "I'm gonna go upstairs, take a shower, and get into something a little more comfortable. I'll call you when I'm ready."

"Sure you don't want me to take a shower with you?" The way she'd been teasing me all night, I was ready to get this party started.

"Ohhh, that sounds nice, but let's stick to the script tonight. I've been planning for a couple of weeks."

"Okay," I agreed, wishing I didn't have to. Sometimes it was hard being the nice guy.

I handed an apple martini to Celeste. She picked up the TV remote and tossed it to me before sashaying toward the stairs, drink in hand. I watched appreciatively. If there was one thing I could say about Celeste, it was that she had one hell of an ass.

I sat on the sofa and turned on the TV, channel surfing until I found an old Muhammad Ali fight on ESPN Classic, but I didn't end up watching any of it. As soon as I set down the remote, I heard my phone ring. It wasn't just any old ring tone either. It was the song "Secret Lovers" by Atlantic Starr—the ring tone I had reserved for Loraine. Once again, her behavior totally caught me off guard. Following me to the men's room, insulting my date, and now calling my phone at one in the morning: These were not the actions of a woman who was done with a relationship.

I stared at the phone, wondering what to do. I mean, I wanted to talk to Loraine to ask her what was really going on. Maybe she was calling to tell me she wanted me back. But then again, she had been pretty pissed off at the club, so maybe she was just calling to curse me out. She probably went home with her minute-man husband, and he left her frustrated once again, so now she was calling out of spite to keep me from getting my groove on with Celeste.

Speaking of Celeste, I heard the shower stop running as I was sitting there deciding whether to answer Loraine's call. My choice was to answer the call from a woman who might be calling just to yell at me or to go upstairs to a woman who was ready to make me feel real good. It was a no-brainer. I hit IGNORE and leaned back on the sofa to watch TV while I waited for Celeste.

Before I could even get into the fight, my phone chirped, letting me know there was a new text message. I didn't have to look at the phone to know who it was from. This was good, though, because now I would know what the hell Loraine wanted without having to speak to her. I could read a text from her without having to mess up my whole night. If she was cursing me out, I could just hit DELETE and be done with it. If it was something else . . . Well, I would decide later how to deal with that. I flipped open my phone to read the text:

I KNOW I SHOULDN'T HAVE ACTED THAT WAY. PLEASE CALL ME BACK. I NEED TO TELL YOU SOMETHING IMPORTANT.

I stared at it for a few seconds, unable to decide what to do. The good news was that she was apologizing for her behavior earlier. The bad news was that she hadn't said enough for me to be able to read between the lines. If only the last line had stopped with "I need you"; then there would be no question about my response. I would be out the door of Celeste's place in a heartbeat. But she hadn't said that, so who knows what the "something important" was? It could have been just about anything—and for that, I wasn't willing to give up what was just beginning between Celeste and me.

If Loraine had something truly important to say, she would have to wait. I sent a reply:

A LITTLE BUSY NOW. I'LL GIVE YOU A CALL IN THE MORNING.

It didn't take long for me to get another text. In fact, I got three in quick succession. The first one read:

THIS CAN'T WAIT UNTIL TOMORROW.

The second one was picture mail. I opened it and saw something I definitely wasn't expecting. It was Loraine in a bathtub, her best features covered by a thick layer of bubbles.

Now she had my complete attention. I read the third message:

I'M AT THE MARRIOTT ALONE. ROOM 1424. THE BUBBLES WON'T LAST UNTIL THE MORNING AND NEITHER WILL I. CALL ME.

My heart was pounding. All night long I'd been trying to figure out what the dramatics were about, and I was afraid to admit to myself that no matter how great Celeste was, I was still hoping Loraine's actions meant that she still cared. Well, holding out on her had forced her to finally just come out and say it in a straightforward, extremely sexy way.

Needless to say, I called her right away.

"You get my texts?" she asked in a voice that made my manhood stand at attention.

"Oh, yeah, I got them."

"I look sexy, don't I?"

She did look good, but I wasn't about to tell her. I had to make sure she wanted me back for the right reasons. "Loraine, why'd you call me? Is this just because you saw me with another woman?"

There was silence on the line for a good thirty seconds, which

I took to mean that she didn't want to admit her answer was yes. "Bye, Loraine. I don't have time for games."

She hurriedly said, "I miss you, Michael. All right? I miss you so much! I want you to come over here and make love to me."

"You still didn't answer my question. Is this just because you're jealous? 'Cause I don't want to start something only to have you kick me to the curb again."

"I need you, Michael," she said quietly. "I love you."

Instinctively, I said, "I love you too."

"So you coming over here? I really need you. I swear I'll make it worth your while."

Back in the day, when I was the lonely fat kid, I never would have dreamed of a night like this, with one beautiful woman upstairs getting ready to make love to me, and another woman, one who I loved, basically promising me the same thing. If this was a sexual fantasy, of course, I'd somehow end up with both of them in bed, but this was real life, and I had to choose.

Taking a leap of faith to trust that she was done playing games, I told Loraine, "Yeah, I'm coming. I just have to take care of something first."

"Just don't make me wait for too long," I heard her say at the same time Celeste called out to me that she was ready for me to meet her upstairs.

I hung up the phone and heaved myself off the couch with a sigh. If only I didn't have a conscience; then I could just slip out now without even saying anything to Celeste.

It felt like the longest walk of my life as I climbed the stairs to Celeste's bedroom. I guess I wasn't moving fast enough for her, because she called out to me two more times before I opened her bedroom door.

The room was pitch-black. "Celeste?" I heard a click and a single high-hat light turned on. She was sitting across the room in a high-back chair, wearing a silk robe. Not far from her chair was something I never would have expected to see, and I had a feeling it was going to make this whole situation even more difficult.

"Hey, handsome. Welcome to Club Celeste." As she stood up

and walked toward a gold stripper pole that extended from the ceiling down to a small stage, I noticed the six-inch high heels she was wearing. "I had this installed last week just for you."

I stared, openmouthed and genuinely unable to speak.

"I highly believe that a woman must be a lady in the streets and a freak in the sheets." She did a quick spin around the pole and then stopped, posing with a seductive smile on her face.

Damn, she went all out, was all I could think. My mouth was still not working.

"Sit on the bed."

I followed her directions automatically, my brain being controlled by my desire at this point.

There was another click, and Lil' Kim and 50 Cent's song "Magic Stick" started to play in surround sound. Celeste slipped off her robe, revealing a fire-engine-red stripper outfit, including a garter and fishnet stockings.

She jumped on the pole like it was her full-time occupation. I was frozen in my spot. I knew what I had come upstairs to do, but she was putting on a damn good show, and I just couldn't make myself turn away. By the time she got finished doing splits and dips, removing parts of her outfit along the way, I was perspiring. When she turned around and started doing the booty clap, I was ready to take off my clothes right then and there to seal the deal.

My original mission was all but forgotten—that is, until I heard the faint sound of "Secret Lovers" playing on my phone again. I reached into my pocket and hit the SILENCE button right before Celeste ended her routine.

I held my breath, trying to calm my racing heart as she stepped off the stage and walked toward me as naked as the day she was born.

"So, what did you think?" She looked down at the bulge between my legs and smiled. Considering how hard she'd made me, there could be no doubt about what I thought.

I tried to think unsexy thoughts, picturing scenes from some goofy Jim Carrey movie I'd seen on TV the other night, in hopes that it would bring me back from the edge of the cliff I was about to jump off of. I wanted Celeste so damn bad, I was seconds away from abandoning my nice-guy persona and throwing her ass on the bed to do all sorts of nasty things with her. Fortunately, thinking about the movie reduced my hard-on just enough to snap me out of it and make me remember the promise I'd made to Loraine.

She took hold of my zipper, but I reached out and stopped her before I lost control again. "Celeste, wait . . ."

Now it was her turn to stand frozen. My reaction was clearly not what she had expected. Can't say I blamed her, though. How many men would say no to what she was offering?

"Um . . ." I didn't even know how to start.

"Oh. My. God," she started, taking a step back. Her seductive swagger was replaced by sudden self-consciousness. She slumped her shoulders and crossed her arms over her naked breasts. "You didn't like it, did you? You think I'm a slut for doing this."

"No, it's not that. It's just—"

"Just what?" she interrupted sharply. "What is your problem?"

I stood up and tried to put my hands on her shoulders, but she stepped back farther, avoiding my touch. The embarrassment on her face was almost painful to watch. It was time to say what I had to say, to put us both out of this misery.

"Do you remember when we first went out, what you told me?"

"No. I told you a lot of things." Her tone was one of annoyance now. She sensed what was happening and wanted to get this over with as quickly as I did.

"Well, you told me if I was . . . if I was ever going to get back with my ex, I should be the one to tell you . . . and . . . well . . ." Atlantic Starr's song started ringing from my pocket again. She looked down at my pants, and the tears that welled in her eyes let me know that she understood who was calling.

I reached into my pocket and silenced the ringer. "Celeste, I'm—"

"Shut up!" she screamed before I could say sorry. I watched

her rush back to the place where her silk robe lay in a puddle on the floor. She threw it over her naked body and then looked at me, tears streaming down her face.

"It's not you; it's me," I started, knowing as I said it that my words would do nothing to soothe her. "You're beautiful, a great woman, probably more than I deserve, but I can't help the fact that I love Loraine. I've been in love with her since I was fourteen."

This was definitely not what she wanted to hear.

"You motherfucker! Get out! Just get the hell out my house!" she screeched, collapsing into the chair she'd been sitting in when I first entered the room. As I walked out, I wished like hell I could rewind to that moment and stop her before she even turned on the music. But I hadn't, and as I left her house to be with Loraine, I hoped I'd be able to erase the sound of Celeste's sobbing from my memory.

Loraine

16

I stepped out of the tub and wrapped one of the plush Marriott towels around my body. It had been almost an hour since I'd sent Michael a picture of myself naked, and he still hadn't shown up. Both times I tried to call, I was sent to voice mail.

I was starting to think I'd made a huge mistake. Michael was probably laid up somewhere right now with that black Barbie he was feeling all over, and they were laughing their asses off at my expense. With the luck I'd had lately, that picture would be all over the Internet by Monday morning.

Still, I didn't regret sending it. I had to take that chance. No sense in sugarcoating it: I'm a classy woman, but I'm extremely jealous and tremendously territorial when it comes to my men. Seeing that woman all over Michael on the dance floor was the equivalent of torture for me. They might as well have just plucked my eyes out. It's a good thing Leon was there; otherwise I might have ripped that wench's weave right out of her head. I didn't even know anything about her, and I hated that bitch. That was *my* man, and I wasn't about to let her have him without a fight.

I glanced over at the clock radio on the nightstand as I lay down across the bed. It was only 2:15 AM, so time was still on my side, and I was not about to give up. I had a good four or five hours to accomplish my goals before Leon woke up.

I know this is going to sound terrible, but when Michael and that tramp left the party, I knew I had to do something, and that meant getting rid of Leon. We'd planned to stay overnight at the hotel for a romantic weekend, but I didn't have time to waste with Leon, even if his performance would be quick. Thanks to Dr. Marshall, it wasn't hard to come up with a plan. She'd prescribed sleeping pills a while back, so I just slipped one of those into his drink. It didn't take long for the mixture of Ambien CR and champagne to take effect. Before I knew it, he was complaining about a headache. Being the attentive wife that I am, I suggested we go upstairs.

By the time we got to our room, Leon was ready to fall out. I waited a half hour to make sure he was asleep and then promptly went down to the front desk and rented another room, using the excuse that my husband's snoring was driving me crazy. I'd been waiting for Michael ever since, and the clock was ticking. Leon would be asleep for only so long.

I was just about to ring Michael's phone again when there was a knock on the door. I jumped up, leaving the towel behind to answer it. Seeing Michael through the peephole, I cracked the door open and pulled him inside.

"I missed you, Michael. And I love you so much."

"I missed you too." His eyes traveled downward, taking in every inch of my naked body. I took hold of his tie and pulled him into my arms.

From that moment on, there was no more reason for words. We let our actions speak for us, kissing and groping like teenagers as we found our way to the bed. I pulled off Michael's tie and undressed him without ever breaking our kiss; then I lay back on the bed and parted my legs, inviting him to take what he'd been deprived of over the past few months. He wasted no time climbing on top and sliding his penis into me.

I had wave after wave of orgasms, feeling pleasure I hadn't had since our breakup. I'm not sure how long we made love, but it damn sure wasn't the minute or two I'd become used to.

Both Michael and I were still breathing hard, and my body was covered in perspiration. I was lying on top of him with my head on his chest. Overall, I wasn't just happy; I was elated. My toes were still curling from the sensation. More importantly, my love for Michael was renewed. During our lovemaking, I'd had momentary regrets about breaking my vows, but the good so outweighed the bad that I quickly dismissed any thought of the fact that I was married. I had finally gotten my groove back, and for the first time in a long time, I felt like a complete woman. That's why I wasn't really sure why I began to cry uncontrollably.

Michael turned me so that he could see my face. "You okay? I didn't hurt you, did I?"

"No, no, not at all." I kissed his chest. "I just realized that I love you so much."

"I love you too." He kissed me, rolling me onto my back and bringing me to orgasm once again.

Three hours later, regrettably, I was getting dressed. Michael was lying on the bed with two pillows propped behind him, watching me as I slipped on my bra and panties. I wanted to just go ahead and slip back into bed with him. Unfortunately, Leon would probably be up in the next hour or so, and I wanted to be in the bed when he woke up.

"So where do we go from here?" Michael asked me as I stepped into my dress. "Are we just going to go back to the way we were, or are you going to leave Leon?"

I felt all of that great after-sex euphoria leave my body, replaced by a cold rush of reality. I spoke firmly and clearly. "I love you, Michael. There is no doubt in my mind about that, but I'm not going to leave my husband for you or anyone else. He's going through a very rough time right now, and I am not the kind of woman who would desert him when he needs me most."

"But what about me?" Michael countered. "I need you."

I put up my hand to stop him before he started begging. "If you can't deal with it, then there is no reason to continue this conversation."

He looked a little taken aback, but I wasn't going to budge. If he didn't understand the rules, this wasn't going to work. And based on the incredible sex we'd just had, I think both of us wanted it to work.

"Looks like I have no choice," he said with a sigh of resignation. "I gotta deal with it."

I leaned in and kissed him, then sat on the bed with my back to him. "Zip me up, would you?" As he fastened my dress, I told him, "I'll make at least two days a week for you, I swear."

"Mmm-hmm." He kissed my shoulder and then patted my ass as I stood up.

I turned to face him. "Just please don't come to my job or my house."

"I won't come to your job, okay?"

"Or my house." I wanted to make sure we were clear.

"Or your house, Loraine."

"All right, then. So, Thursday is a good day, because that's when Leon goes to therapy. And I can be out all day Sunday, because he's usually out playing golf and he thinks I'm at church all day."

"What if I want more time with you?" Michael challenged, reaching for my hand and pulling me back toward him. I leaned over and kissed him on the mouth.

"This isn't a negotiation, Michael. If Leon catches us, he *might* kill you, but he'd definitely kill me."

Michael pouted for a minute while I stood there fidgeting. I needed to end this conversation and get back to my room before Leon woke up, but I could tell Michael was still dissatisfied. I needed us to be on the same page before I could go. If he was unhappy, he might do something rash, like confront Leon and tell him about tonight.

"So, we're okay, right?" I asked cautiously.

"Okay," Michael relented, and then he blindsided me with a request I never saw coming. "But if you get to be with Leon, do I get to be with Celeste?"

For a second I wanted to slap his ass, but then I realized what he was doing: He was trying to force my hand. He thought that if he made me jealous with Celeste, I would change the rules and leave Leon. I was not about to be played like that. He was going to have to choose. It was either me or her.

"Oh, so you want to be with her? Is that what you wanna do? Well, motherfucker, go be with her ass, then!" I knelt down and peered under the bed. "Where the hell are my shoes? I need to get the fuck away from you."

"Loraine, calm down." He jumped off the bed and knelt down beside me. "I was just trying to make a point."

"Well, that ain't a damn point you wanna make around me." I stood up and slipped my foot into my shoe.

He placed his hands on my arms to stop my frantic movement, and forced me to look in his eyes. "If I wanted to be with her, I wouldn't be here now. I love you, babe, not her."

I was so upset I was shaking. "Michael, I need to know I'm going to be the only woman you sleep with."

"You are. But I need you to understand why I want you all to myself. How am I supposed to know that you're not gonna wake up one day and dump me again? I've got feelings, too, Loraine."

"I promise that will never happen again."

"I hope not, because if it does, I'm not going to be responsible for my actions."

There was a certain edge to his words that I'd never heard before. I knew Michael would never hurt a fly, but there was something about how he spoke that didn't set right with my spirit. I just hoped I never found out what it was.

Jerome

17

After my dramatic run-in with Big Poppa, I was feeling much better than I would have expected. I had lived my life in limbo for so long, waiting for him to love me and only me, that now that I'd finally put a stop to it, I was feeling a surprising sense of freedom. Like I had given myself permission to move on with my life.

I was feeling so great that I pushed up the timetable on a project I'd been working on for a while. I had been making some calls on Ron's behalf to see about him playing basketball overseas. Through a friend of a friend, I had managed to get a video of Ron's skills seen by the coach of a team in the Ligue Nationale de Basket, France's equivalent of the NBA. The coach liked what he saw and pretty much told me that a tryout was just a formality. If Ron wanted his career back, it was his for the taking.

I told the coach I would have Ron call and arrange a visit. But now that I was free of my entanglement with Big Poppa, I did something spontaneous: I stopped at a travel agency and bought us first-class tickets to France and three weeks' accommodations at one of the finest hotels in Paris. He could meet with the coach, and then we could spend a few weeks celebrating in high style.

As I pulled up in front of the hotel, I couldn't wait to get inside and tell him the good news. I was hoping that this would make him happy, because that's what having him in my life did for me—Ron made me very happy.

"Welcome back, sir."

I was greeted by the young man at the reservations desk, but his polite words were not matched by the expression on his face. I couldn't quite put my finger on it, but there was a weird vibe coming from him and from the bellhop standing near him. The bellhop turned away as I approached, but not before I caught the smirk on his face.

I had an inkling that I knew what was going on, but I had to test my theory. I held up the bag of Mexican food and said, "Just bringing back food for me and my son." Ever since we checked in, Ron and I had given everyone the impression that we were father and son. Ron still wasn't ready to leave behind his down-low comfort zone.

The young man's reaction let me know that I was correct; our cover was blown.

"Uh, yeah, about that, sir . . ."

I placed the food on the counter and looked at him with eyes that dared him to say the wrong thing.

"Well, first I wanna say that you and your friend don't have anything to be ashamed of. I have two brothers who are gay."

I didn't give a shit about his brothers. I just wanted to know how he knew the truth about me and Ron, because I was pretty damn sure that Ron hadn't been the one to tell him.

When I didn't respond to him, he seemed to get even more nervous. At this point, the bellhop disappeared from behind the desk. He probably didn't want to be anywhere near this conversation, because if this kid said the wrong thing to me, at least one of them was losing his job tonight.

"Yeah, well, anyway . . . um . . . I saw your friend coming back in earlier, and I said some things that might have upset him."

I was still lost. The things this kid said were sending up so many red flags, I didn't even know where to start. "Wait. Did you say he was coming back in? From where?"

"I'm not really sure, but he did ask me earlier for directions to the nearest post office."

This made no sense at all, but I would ask Ron about that when I got back to the room. In the meantime, I asked the kid, "Okay, so what did you say that upset him?"

"Well, it wasn't really what I said. I showed him this." He reached under the counter to retrieve a newspaper, and slid it across the counter to me. "I just thought he should know about it."

I picked up the paper, which was folded open to an article that nearly caused me to shit myself. There was a picture of Ron and me holding hands, along with a blurred version of the explicit photos Peter had taken last year. The headline read: FALLEN HERO: LOCAL BASKETBALL STAR QUITS SCHOOL TO BE WITH OLDER GAY LOVER.

I threw the paper back on the counter and looked up at the desk clerk, feeling close to tears and wanting answers that no one could give me. I wanted to know why Peter wouldn't leave me the hell alone. I wanted to know why Ron and I couldn't just get on with our lives without all this drama. I wanted to know why the clerk had shown this to Ron when I wasn't there to comfort him.

That's when I realized what all of Ron's calls had been about earlier. He had seen the article and wanted to tell me. And I hadn't been there when he needed me most. Shit.

"I'm really sorry, sir," the clerk called after me, but I was already running for the elevator.

My stomach was in knots as I slid the card into the slot to unlock our door. The last time Ron had been humiliated by Peter, he nearly broke my jaw. For all I knew, he was waiting to hit me now, but I couldn't stop to worry about that. We were so close to happiness; I just had to fix this situation as quickly as I could.

With my hand on the doorknob, I took a few deep breaths to try to calm myself. *Everything is all right,* I told myself before going in. *We're going to Europe. He's going to play ball, and I'm going to start an import/export business. We will not let this stop us.*

I stepped inside the room, which was dimly lit. The bed was unmade but empty. "Ron?" I called to him as I headed to the bathroom, the only other place he could be.

The door was shut. I called his name again but got no answer. "Hey, Ron, look. I know about what you saw in the paper, but it's okay. We're gonna get through this." There was still no response. "Hey, you. Come on out and talk to me. I have a surprise that will make all of this better."

When he still wouldn't speak to me, I opened the door and went into the bathroom. What I saw turned my legs to jelly. I feel hard on my knees to the tile floor.

Ron was lying in the tub, his long legs bent into an uncomfortable position. His eyes were open, but heavy-lidded and vacant. A small trail of dried saliva traveled from his mouth down to his chin. His arm was splayed to the side, his hand hanging over the tub, almost like he was directing me to look at what he'd left on the floor. There were two prescription bottles, the medicines he'd been prescribed for his depression and anxiety after quitting basketball. Both bottles were empty.

"Oh, God! No!" I cried out as I crawled across the floor to reach him. "No, no, no, Ron!" I put a hand on his chest. It was motionless and cold. He was gone. "You didn't have to do this. Jesus Christ, you didn't have to do this," I wailed. "I was gonna take you away from all this."

I sat slumped on the bathroom floor for a long time, trying to come to terms with reality. Every time I looked at Ron's body, I'd imagine him stepping out of the tub and then the two of us packing our bags and leaving for Europe that night. I replayed happy times with Ron in my mind, and cried until I had no more tears left. Then I just sat and stared silently at Ron's body, not wanting to believe he was gone.

I knew Ron had had his depressed moments, and sure, he'd talked about not wanting to be here anymore, but I thought things were looking up. The last few weeks he'd seemed like his old self. I never dreamed he was capable of taking his own life. But then again, that was before Peter tracked us down again.

"Nooooooooo!" The sound came out more like a roar than actual words. If I had never met Peter, this never would have happened to Ron. I was responsible for his death. As I finally pulled myself off the floor to call 911, I wondered how I would ever be able to live with myself.

Leon

18

When I showed up for therapy at my usual time, Roberta's receptionist informed me that she'd had to leave unexpectedly and that we would have to reschedule. Her eight-year-old son had fallen on the school playground and broken his arm, so Roberta was with him in the emergency room. I was sorry to hear that, but I wasn't stressing it at all. To tell you the truth, I was thinking about cutting back our twice-weekly therapy sessions to once a week anyway. Things were just getting too intense as of late, and I wasn't sure I could take much more. They called it therapy, but to me it was starting to become more like torture.

I'd originally come to see Roberta for help with my marriage and sexual shortcomings, but now I was coming face-to-face with issues and secrets that probably should have just remained buried. In our last few sessions, she had me talking about stuff that was just way too close to home and totally off topic, as far as I was concerned, not to mention none of her business. Besides, things between Loraine and me had gotten so much better now that we'd had our conversation about my aunt. Where I thought she would be appalled, she actually embraced me, and I was grateful for her love and support. Sure, there was still the premature-ejaculation issue, but now that she knew where the root of the issue lay, she actually seemed relieved. I guess she felt better knowing that it wasn't something wrong with her. It's funny what peace of mind can do, because lately she'd been humming and singing like all her frustrations had been swept away in one night. If she wasn't so close to menopause, I'd swear she was pregnant because lately she almost glowed.

On the way home from Roberta's office, traffic was so backed up that I decided to take back roads home and pick up some Chinese food from this place on Parham Road that the whole town seemed to be raving about. I'd wanted to bring Loraine there, considering how much she loved Chinese, but it would have to be another day.

I'd spoken to her about a half hour ago, and she told me she had some big dinner meeting up in Fredericksburg with a client. Unfortunately, she wouldn't be home until sometime around eleven, so I'd be eating shrimp and broccoli and egg rolls by myself.

As I sat at the light waiting to make the turn into the Chinese restaurant, I thought my eyes were playing tricks on me, because across the street, pulling out of the restaurant parking lot, I saw the prettiest metallic-blue Cadillac. Now, I'll be the first to admit I like the new Caddies, but it wasn't the car that almost made me break my neck doing a double take. It was the woman sitting in the passenger's seat. I swear she looked just like my wife. Of course, she couldn't be, because Loraine was in Fredericksburg at a meeting.

I watched the Caddie pull out and disappear in the traffic down Parham Road. Now, call it a hunch, a gut feeling, psychic abilities, or just plain curiosity, but when the light turned green, something told me to follow that car instead of going to the restaurant. I drove for almost a mile before I was able to catch up to the Caddie, and when I did, I almost slammed into the back of the car in front of me because I was staring so hard at the Cadillac. The driver made a left turn, and I was able to get a better look at the passenger. She didn't just look like my wife. That woman *was* my wife! My stomach plummeted like an elevator with a broken cable, and my heart pounded in my chest like a jackhammer. To make matters worse, there was no doubt in my mind that the guy driving the car was that son of a bitch she used to mess with. I cut off two other drivers to make a quick left, leaving a trail of blaring horns behind me.

Another half mile or so down the road, I caught up with them again. They clearly had no idea I was behind them, because Loraine was leaning on him and kissing his neck.

So much for our little celibacy pact. Now I knew why her mood had changed and she was so damn happy all the time. While I was in therapy, she was out on the street getting a little sexual healing. Jealousy and rage coursed through my body, escaping through my fist as I pounded the steering wheel.

I thought about plowing my car into the back of Michael's Caddie, but the hand of reason held me back. Instead, I continued to follow them—for what, I wasn't sure quite yet.

I knew there was a good possibility that they were headed to a motel, and as I envisioned the confrontation we would have in the parking lot, I did a quick mental inventory of the contents of my trunk. My golf clubs were still in there. Perfect. By the time I got through with him, Michael's face would be bruised the same shade of blue as his Cadillac, and his car would need more body work than he could ever afford.

I smiled as I imagined myself swinging a nine iron into the windshield of his shiny car, but the feeling was only temporary. As I trailed a few cars behind them, I could see Loraine's hands waving all over the place, the way they often did when she was talking excitedly. Oh, she was all comfortable and cozy with this dude. Suddenly, I couldn't handle this ruse any longer. I couldn't take another minute.

At the next red light, I swerved around another car and screeched to a halt alongside them, blowing my horn like I'd lost my fucking mind. Michael and Loraine looked in the direction of the sound, at first appearing angry, like they were going to tell someone off for honking at them. But when she realized who she was looking at, Loraine's eyes widened and her mouth flew open. She put her hand over her mouth.

"That's right, bitch! You been busted!" I screamed as I lowered my window. "Get out that car," I hollered, pointing my finger at her. "Get out the fucking car!"

I could read Loraine's lips: *Oh my God.*

"Is that all you got to say? Get the hell over here RIGHT NOW!" I opened my car door and stepped out. By now, the light had changed, and the driver behind Michael leaned on his horn. Michael moved his car forward. For a second I thought that punk was going to drive away and make me chase him like a maniac through the streets of Richmond, but suprisingly he acted like he had some sense, pulling over to the side of the road.

A few more drivers honked their horns, signaling for me to move, but I just flipped them off. There was plenty of room for them to drive around my car. I had more important things to take care of.

I could see some conversation going on between them as I approached his car. Loraine touched Michael's shoulder as if to say, *Don't do anything. Please don't do anything.* Hmph. She just didn't know. I was ready to beat Michael's ass right there in the middle of the street.

I was about to bang on the windows, but Loraine came to her senses and got out of the car. She didn't even look at me. She just scooted out of Michael's car, walked around to mine, and climbed into the passenger's seat. She had barely gotten her leg in the door when I jumped in and sped off with a lurch.

"I should whip your fucking ass!" I hollered at her. "I don't believe this shit. Here I am going through therapy, trying to keep our marriage together, and you out messing with this man."

I was surprised at how calm her voice remained. "Leon, it's not what you think."

"Oh, it's not? Well, then, why don't you fucking enlighten me!"

"We were just having a business meeting. He just wanted to talk to me about some business."

Was this bitch for real, or did she just think I was the dumbest motherfucker on Earth? A business meeting with a dude she used to fuck.

"Business, huh? I thought you had a business meeting in Fredericksburg with Mary Dupree. If I remember correctly, you was just getting off at her exit." She didn't have much to say about that. "I can't believe you could do me like this."

"I'm sorry, Leon. But you gotta believe me; I wasn't gonna do anything with him. You got this whole thing wrong. I love you, baby, and only you."

I turned my head completely in her direction. "If you don't shut your lying-ass mouth, I'm gonna slap your ass to next week. Now, try my ass if you want to." It had been a long time since an argument had escalated to this level, but I was done with this whole calm, cool, and collected "let's talk this out" shit. I mean, look how far it had gotten me: a wife who was walking all over me.

I turned my attention back to the road. "We're gonna finish this conversation when we get home."

I drove the rest of the way in silence. I was so blinded by rage that I don't know how I made it home without running a red light or running someone over.

As soon as I stomped into my house, I went straight for the bar in the family room, where I poured myself a healthy glass of Hennessey. I didn't know what I was going to do. I was two seconds away from whipping Loraine's ass when she came in the house, only I was scared that if I did, I might push her into that bastard's arms for good. As fucked up as it was, I still loved her.

"Leon."

Loraine came into the family room, looking all guilty. I think she was expecting to get her ass beat, but still, she was holding her head up like she hadn't done anything. It was as if she'd declared, *This is my story, and I'm sticking to it.*

I gulped down my drink and took a deep breath, trying to control my fury. "You want a divorce? You want me to move out?"

She stared at me in shock. "No, this is our house, and you're my husband. Neither one of us is going anywhere."

I poured another drink. "So you gonna tell me what I did to deserve this? 'Cause you told me sex wasn't that important if two people had love."

"You don't deserve this at all. This is all my fault, but it's all a big misunderstanding."

"You damn right it's your fault. All I wanna know is how long have you been fucking his ass?"

"Leon, I haven't—"

Before she could spit out another lie, the doorbell rang.

"Who the hell is that?" I bellowed, thinking that whoever it was had a pretty good chance of getting punched in the mouth if they said the slightest thing to piss me off.

Loraine

19

I couldn't stop my body from trembling as I watched Leon stomp into the house. I stood outside, cursing myself for being so stupid. Dammit, was I ever going to catch a break? I still couldn't believe he'd caught Michael and me together. He wasn't even supposed to be on that side of town. He was supposed to be at therapy. Why the hell did I push Michael so hard to take me to that Chinese restaurant? If I had just listened to him, we'd be up in the Marriott getting our groove on right now with a lot less drama.

I stayed out there for a while, trying to gather the courage to go into the house. Leon and I had gotten into our share of domestic altercations over the years, but it had been me who couldn't control my temper. I'd always lashed out at him first. This time, he was madder than I think I'd ever seen him, and I had a feeling the situation could get dangerous. I'm not gonna lie; I was so afraid of what he might do that I considered running. But it was my carelessness that had gotten me into this mess, and now I had to go inside to try to clean it up.

Don't get me wrong; I felt bad that Leon's feelings were hurt. But right now, my first priority was to calm him down so no one—not me, not Leon, and not Michael—got physically hurt. If that meant going in there and lying my ass off, then that's what I would do.

Who knew where my marriage stood now. I didn't want it to be over—I knew that much—but now that I was back with Michael, I didn't want to give him up either. Somewhere in the back of my mind, I'd known I would eventually have to make a choice, but dammit, I wasn't ready to make it yet. As I stumbled up the walkway on shaky legs, I had no idea which way this conversation would go. All I knew was I had to start somewhere, preferably without violence.

In the living room, Leon was pouring himself a drink. I wanted to tell him to move over and pour me one, too, but I needed a clear head if I was going to talk my way out of this one.

I kept a safe distance away from Leon as he finished his first drink. A bit of the tension seemed to leave his shoulders as he poured himself another, and I figured it was safe to start talking.

"Leon." I took a few cautious steps closer to him. I'd already mapped out my escape route to the bathroom if things suddenly got out of hand. My heart felt like it was trying to push its way out of my chest, but I used every trick I'd ever learned in the business world to practice the art of "never let them see you sweat." I needed Leon to believe I was calm. Only an innocent woman would be calm in a situation like this, right?

"You want a divorce?" he asked. "You want me to move out?"

His words threw me off for a second, but something behind his eyes told me he didn't really want me to answer yes. I felt a glimmer of hope.

"No," I told him, "this is our house, and you're my husband. Neither one of us is going anywhere."

His hands were unsteady as he poured another drink. "So you gonna tell me what I did to deserve this? 'Cause you told me sex wasn't that important if two people had love."

We went back and forth a few more times, with him accusing me of lying and me swearing that everything was all a big misunderstanding. This approach was clearly getting us nowhere. He was hurting, and not ready to let go of it yet. He didn't want to believe I could be innocent.

Then I had a brilliant idea. It was time for me to go to therapy. Not that I felt like I had any problems—certainly nothing as serious as Leon's past—that needed to be worked out; I just knew that offering to see a therapist would stop this conversation in its tracks and buy me some more time.

I was about to offer this solution when I was interrupted by the ringing doorbell.

"Who the hell is that?" he snapped.

He started to come out from behind the bar, but I stopped him. Thinking fast, I handed him the bottle of Hennessey. "Look, I'll get the door. You just try and calm yourself down. Have another drink."

"That better not be that nigga!"

That's exactly what I was afraid of.

"He's not stupid," I said, praying I was right. "Why would he come here?" I trudged to the door, hoping it was UPS with some of the HSN stuff I'd ordered.

You guessed it. It was Michael standing on the other side of the door, and I had to put my hand up to stop him from rushing into my house as soon as I opened the door.

I stepped outside and shut the door behind me. "Michael, what the hell are you doing here? I told you I could handle this."

I looked down at his hands, which were shoved into his pockets, and it scared the crap out of me. "Oh, no," I gasped. When Leon first pulled up beside us, yelling and screaming, Michael shocked the hell out of me by pulling a gun out of his glove compartment. Would you believe he was about to get out of the car and confront Leon with it? I had to beg him to put it away and let me get out of the car alone.

I looked into his eyes, searching for a sign of his intentions. Did he plan on using that gun now? I took his arms and pulled him down two steps to the walkway, as if it would make a difference to get him that little bit farther away from my front door. "Michael, what are you doing here?"

"I just came to see if you were all right." He pulled his hands out of his pockets, with no gun in sight. That made me feel a little better, but I still needed to get him out of there in a hurry.

"I told you I'd call you when I got a chance."

"That was half an hour ago. He could have killed you by now."

"Well, I'm not dead yet, but if you don't get out of here, I will be. You're only making things worse by being here."

"Look, I don't want you to stay here tonight. That guy's unstable. He didn't hit you or anything, did he?"

"I'm fine, Michael. Please, you have to go. I can handle this. I'll call you later. I promise."

"You promise!"

I could feel a rush of air as Leon opened the door behind me. He saw Michael and went ballistic. I ran up the steps and shoved my hands hard against his chest to stop him from going any farther. I planted my feet firmly on the ground, struggling to stay upright as Leon grabbed my shoulders in a painfully tight grip.

"You fucking disrespectful bitch! I know you ain't got this nigga standing outside my house, talking to you like I ain't even here!"

"Leon, this is not what it looks like."

"What do you think, I'm fucking blind? This is exactly what it looks like. This high-yellow nigga just followed us home! But that's all right. I'm gonna put a cap in your ass, nigga, and the law won't say a thing, because you trespassing."

Leon was talking a lot of shit for a man who didn't own a gun, and I was scared Michael might put him in his place by pulling out a real weapon.

Fortunately, he restrained himself, only issuing a warning. "Loraine, you best tell this man to stop threatening me or you'll be burying him instead of divorcing him."

"Oh, God." I could feel it; we were only seconds away from some real tragedy. I kept my hands on Leon's chest but craned my neck around to speak to Michael. "Please don't do anything stupid. Just get outta here. Please!"

"Get out my way! I ain't scared of that punk-ass motherfucker." I had both arms wrapped around Leon's waist at this point, but he was still inching closer to Michael. "What's wrong, sissy boy? You hiding behind a woman because you afraid you gonna get your ass whipped by a real man?"

Michael laughed. "I know you didn't just call me a sissy and challenge my manhood, Minute Man."

It took a second, but when Michael's words sunk in, I no longer had to restrain Leon. All the fight went out of him like a deflated balloon. He was defeated without even one punch being thrown.

"What did you call me?"

"You heard me, Johnny Quick. I probably wouldn't be here if you could last more than a minute or two."

I turned and screamed, "Michael, shut up!"

Leon was looking at me with tears glistening in his eyes. "How could you? How could you tell him, of all people, about our . . . my personal business?"

"Leon, I . . . I . . ." I couldn't answer because I didn't know what to say. Michael had straight up put me out there, whether or not he'd done it on purpose.

"You want her, you can have her," Leon said, pushing me toward Michael.

I tried to wrap my arms around him, but he slapped my hands away. "Leon, please don't do this."

"Loraine, come on," Michael said from the walkway. "You heard the man. He don't want you."

I spun around, looking Michael dead in the eyes. "Get out of here! Get the fuck outta here! Nobody asked you to come here."

I turned back to Leon, pleading, "Baby, please. I'm sorry. Don't do this. He doesn't mean anything to me!"

"I may have issues, but I don't want your pity. I do have some pride. I'll have my lawyer draw up some papers." He turned to go into the house.

"No," I screamed. "I don't want no fucking divorce!" I refused to believe that things had really reached this point.

Leon stopped and turned around, and when I saw the look in his eyes, I knew that whether or not I liked it, I had to make a choice. His eyes weren't filled with tears anymore. "What about him? You ready to give him up?" He pointed at Michael.

"I'll do whatever it takes. You're my husband; he's not. We took an oath to be together for better or for worse, till death do us part." I couldn't, wouldn't, look back at Michael, because unfortunately, I meant every word of what I had said.

"Then get your ass in the house. This shit ain't over yet." I couldn't tell if the threat was directed at me, because he was looking at Michael as he spoke. "Now you can get the hell off my property. Your services are no longer needed."

"Loraine," Michael called out one last time.

"Go home, Michael, and please don't try to contact me again. I don't want to hurt my husband any more than I have." With that being said, I walked in the house to deal with the consequences of my actions.

Michael

20

I pulled into the parking lot across from Loraine's office building and picked up my cell phone to dial her private line. It was Monday afternoon, four days after Leon had busted us. I felt like I was about to lose my mind, because I still hadn't heard from Loraine. I'd thought I was doing the right thing by giving her some time to make nice with that psychopath husband. I knew she didn't mean any of those horrible things she had said to me; she was just putting on a show for Leon. I figured she'd give me a call the first chance she got. At least that's what I thought; until I called her cell phone Sunday night and found out she'd changed her number.

"Loraine Farrow's line." I was surprised to hear her secretary's voice. Hannah never answered this line.

"Can I speak to Mrs. Farrow, please?"

"Sure. May I tell her who's calling?"

"Ah, yes, can you tell her it's Michael?" Well, at least it appeared she was in the office.

Hannah put me on hold for a minute. I expected to hear Loraine's voice, but it was Hannah who returned and said, "Sir, Mrs. Farrow has asked me to tell you not to call here again. In fact, she would really appreciate it if you would not try to contact her at all."

I tried to maintain my composure, even as I issued an ultimatum. "Listen, I know you just work for her and you're doing what you're told, but please tell Mrs. Farrow that if she doesn't have time to speak to me by phone, I'll have no choice but to come to her office and wait until she has time."

Once again, she put me on hold. A few minutes later, another voice came on the line. "Sir, my name is Greg Wilkins with building security. I'm here to inform you that if you make any attempt to enter the premises, you will be arrested for trespassing. I have also advised Mrs. Farrow that if she receives any more calls from you, I will assist her in filing harassment charges."

"This is bull. All I wanna do is talk to her."

"Well, I think it's pretty obvious she doesn't want to talk to you, sir."

"I don't fucking believe this. Tell Mrs. Farrow life ain't worth living if I can't live it with her."

"Again, sir, if you come on the premises, you will be arrested."

I hung up. "Fucking rent-a-cop."

I had half a mind to go up in that building and force Loraine to talk to me, but my life was fucked up enough at the moment. The last thing I needed was an arrest on top of everything else. I drove down to a secluded section of the James River to think things through. This was where I went whenever I needed to get my head together. There was something about the sound of the river that made me think clearer.

Truth be told, I knew I'd been acting a little crazy lately, but what could I do? I loved Loraine more than I'd ever loved anyone in my entire life. I just wanted us to be happy, like we were before she took back that husband of hers. Dammit, why the hell wouldn't she just leave his ass?

I slammed my hand into the steering wheel. "Stupid! Stupid! Stupid!" I screamed at myself. I should have known she would do this. I should have ignored her texts and kept my ass at Celeste's house. I'd be having private pole dances every night, instead of this constant bullshit from a woman who couldn't make up her mind.

I didn't want to accept the fact that loving Loraine was nothing more than a dead-end road, but I was starting to think it was a real possibility. She never had any intention of leaving Leon. I'd always thought that we'd grow old together, but the way she had things planned, I'd be eighty years old and waiting until Leon left to go play shuffleboard before I could see her.

That's when I came to the conclusion that there was only one way Loraine and I were ever really going to be together. That's also when I decided to get rid of the competition, because as long as Leon was in the picture, I really had no chance. The only real question was if I had what it takes to get rid of the bastard.

I opened my glove compartment and took out my gun, admiring it as I stepped out of the car. I pointed it at a tree and pulled the trigger, letting off three rounds. All three bullets landed squarely in the middle of the tree, just where I had aimed. I let out a loud laugh. If the tree had been a man, he'd be dead right now. I had to admit, I'd become a pretty good shot.

Jerome

21

The cab pulled up in front of my house, and the driver stepped out to retrieve my bags from the trunk. I'd been away for a little more than a month on what you might call a soul-searching mission. I'd cashed in the tickets I'd purchased for Ron and me to go to France in exchange for a single ticket to St. Thomas in the U.S. Virgin Islands and a suite at the Marriott Frenchman's Reef.

I was hoping that the time away would help me get over Ron, but the truth was that after a month, I was coming home almost as messed up as I'd been when I left. Well, maybe not quite as bad. I was a total basket case my first week there. Out of respect for his mother, I didn't attend his funeral, so I felt like I never got a chance to say good-bye. Part of me didn't even feel like I deserved that chance, though, because I still blamed myself for his death.

After the first week, I found the strength to get out of bed and spend some time by the pool at the hotel, but there was no joy in anything I did. I barely spoke to anyone. I spent most of my time peeking around corners, like I half expected to see Peter there, smirking at me.

I slid the key in my front door with a sigh, wondering if I would ever get over Ron's death.

"So you're back?"

I jumped back and dropped my suitcase when I heard the voice come from my dimly lit living room. My first thought was shit, Peter had gotten in my house. It took a minute for my pulse to slow down and my brain to process the fact that I recognized

the voice, and it wasn't Peter. Big Poppa was lounging in my living room like he didn't have a care in the world.

I stepped inside and flicked on the high hats, flooding the
room with light. I hadn't seen Big Poppa in two months, and although he looked a little haggard, my heart still skipped a beat
at the sight of him. Say whatever you want about the man, but
you couldn't take anything from his looks. He was one fine male
specimen. Old boy actually looked happy to see me too. I wasn't
sure yet how I felt about seeing him.

"What are you doing here?" I didn't have to ask how he'd
gotten in. With everything going on with Ron, I hadn't had time
to change my locks before I left.

"Reminiscing, I guess." He stood up and held out his open
palms, giving me this imploring, kind of pitiful look, one I'd
never seen on his face before. "I was having a rough day. Whenever I'm feeling a little low, which seems to be every day lately, I
come over here and pour myself a drink. I got good memories of
this place. Usually makes me feel better. I hope you don't mind."

"No, it's cool," I said, and I actually meant it. "But I'm still
gonna need those keys before you leave." A quick glance around
my clean apartment told me he hadn't done anything but hang
out, but Peter had taught me that you never could predict who
would go off the deep end into Crazyville.

I took off my coat and hung it on the back of a chair, then
went to sit on the couch. "So what's going on? You're not the
type to be going through depression."

"A lot of things." Big Poppa let out a deep sigh as he sat
down next to me. "Work sucks, my wife's a bitch, but mostly
I've been missing you."

"That's nice," I said. Once upon a time, those words would
have meant so much to me. Now I couldn't even return the sen-
timent.

"So how have you been?" he asked awkwardly. "I've tried to
call you, and you never answer the phone."

"I've been all right, I guess. I was down in the Islands for the
past month."

"Wow, a month. That's a long trip."

"Yeah, I was trying to get some R and R. My friend, the guy I was seeing, he passed away."

"Yeah, man, that was part of the reason I was trying to get in contact with you. I read in the newspaper about what happened. I wanted to offer my condolences."

"Thanks. He was a good man." I turned to look at Big Poppa, and surprisingly, I didn't detect any jealousy. "So you know about what happened, huh?"

"Uh-huh. They had your picture plastered all over the newspaper. I didn't know what to think."

"Don't believe everything you read in the newspaper. I have a suspicion that I know who wrote the article: that guy who's been stalking me."

"Damn, I didn't even think about that. You really need to do something about that guy."

"You think I don't know that?" I snapped.

Big Poppa got off that subject quick. "They said that dude committed suicide. Is that true?"

"Yeah, it's true. I found him." I nodded sadly.

"Jerome, I'm really sorry, man. He was just a kid."

"Yep, he just turned twenty." Every time I thought about how young and innocent Ron was, I started tearing up. I couldn't talk about this anymore. "So what about you? Why are you really here?"

"Like I said, I miss you." He reached for my hand, but I slid it out of the way. I wasn't ready for that. "I've been coming here every couple of days for the past few weeks, hoping one day you'd come home. And here you are."

"Yep, here I am," I said flatly. I had nothing else to give him; I felt empty inside.

Big Poppa sighed. "Look, I know you're still grieving this young man's death—"

I cut him off. "Ron. His name was Ron."

"Ron, yeah, sorry. I know you're still grieving Ron's death. And there were a lot of things said last time we spoke, but is there any chance of us getting back together? I really do miss you, Jerome."

I sat there studying his face for a second. He looked so good.

It would have been so easy to lean across the coffee table and tongue him down, initiating a very steamy lovemaking session right there in my living room. I hadn't made love since the morning of Ron's death. Until now, I hadn't even thought about it, despite all the down-low brothers who'd tried to talk to me down in St. Thomas. I wanted to say yes so bad, if just for the sex, but I'd be lying to myself if I said I was ready to date this man again.

"It's tempting, more tempting than you will ever know, but I'm sorry. I can't do it. Not right now."

He looked surprised, perhaps even hurt. "Can't, or won't?"

"Both," I said with finality. "I start messing around with you, I'll never find Mr. Right."

"What if I'm Mr. Right?"

"We've already had this argument. You are not Mr. Right; you're Mr. Right Now. You can't give me what I need."

He grabbed his crotch. "I've got what you need right here. I always have."

"You know, it's a damn shame," I said with a wry laugh. "How long we been messing with each other? What, almost six years? And you still think it's about the dick."

He looked at me with his eyebrows scrunched up, as if to say *What else is there?*

I shook my head. "Ain't gonna be much fucking when we're both seventy years old."

"Jerome, what do you want from me?"

"I want what you can't give. I want something long-term. I want to take care of you and watch you get old. I want to be there when you're sick and all alone." I got up from my seat and picked up my suitcase. "It was good seeing you, Poppa. I'm gonna go and unpack. Leave your key on the counter on your way out."

Leon

22

"Leon, I didn't think you were going to make it."

I walked into Roberta's office twenty minutes late for my appointment after spending the afternoon at Loraine's office, setting up a webcam and some spyware on her computer. It might sound a little over the top to be spying on my wife like that, but after catching her with Michael, I didn't feel like I could trust her. She doesn't like the idea, but that's her problem. The spy gear would ensure that I was never caught off guard like that again. Still, as I installed everything, and she looked on, I knew this wasn't the best way to keep my marriage intact. If I couldn't trust my wife, there wasn't much hope for us. Maybe a little time with Roberta would help me get my mind right and get past this.

"You're lucky I even showed up with all the shit I had to deal with this weekend." I sat down in the reclining chair in front of her. I'm sure I looked like shit, because I hadn't slept more than a few hours since last Thursday night when I busted them.

"What happened?" She picked up her notebook and a pen.

"Plain and simple: I caught Loraine cheating on me."

"Leon, I'm sorry. I know how much you've been trying to work on your marriage."

"Oh, let's not even go there, because she had the nerve to be using the time I spend here to be seeing the motherfucker."

She put down the pen and looked at me for a long moment, probably trying to restrain herself from saying what she really felt about Loraine. I always wondered how therapists managed to keep from stating their personal feelings. In Roberta's case, she would just ask another question.

"Was it the same man you'd been concerned about?"

"Yeah, it was that motherfucker. Roberta, I swear I wanted to kill him."

"What about Loraine? What does she say about all this?"

"Oh, she's so sorry," I said, my tone edged with sarcasm. "She just wants to work it out. I'm surprised she didn't call you for an appointment."

"No, I haven't heard from her . . . yet. But what about you? Do you want to work it out?"

"I don't know. I love her, but she's fucked me up pretty good this time. I don't know if it's possible."

"Couples have affairs and survive them, if they are willing to work on the marriage to save it. The real question is do you want to save it, Leon?" She gave me a pointed look. Good old Roberta; she never would take "I don't know" as an answer.

"I don't know if I'll ever trust her again," I admitted, thinking of the camera I'd just installed. "Every time I think of her being with him, I just want to scream." I slammed my hand down on the arm of the chair.

"I know you're upset, but you have to stay calm."

"Roberta, that son of a bitch came to my house. How am I supposed to stay calm when my mind is full of stuff like that?"

Roberta peered over her glasses at me and stared me down. I knew exactly what she was doing. She wasn't the type of woman to say things twice. She would sit there and look at me like that until I calmed down. No sense in prolonging the stare; I folded my hands in my lap to let her know I'd heard her and that she could continue.

"I told you this was going to happen," I said bitterly.

"Yes, you did."

"And it's going to happen again. Loraine's going to sleep with him again if you don't help me, Roberta. You gotta find a way to stop me from finishing so quick. If I can't please my wife, she's gonna keep finding someone else to do it." I was reaching a point of desperation. All this work I'd been doing in therapy and I still hadn't accomplished a damn thing except digging up old memories. I wanted a quick fix, because with Loraine's cheating ass, I felt like the clock was ticking on my marriage.

"We're going to find a way, Leon. I promise you we're going to find a way."

"Yeah," I scoffed. "That's what you keep saying, but so far I don't see a damn thing changed."

For a quick second, her eyes narrowed and her mouth tightened, like she wanted to curse me out for questioning her ability as a therapist. "Well," she started, "perhaps there's another reason that things aren't progressing as quickly as you'd like."

"What are you talking about?" If she was about to suggest another hypnosis session, I just might have to find a new therapist.

"You've got much bigger problems we should be dealing with if you're going to have a healthy marriage."

"What are you talking about?" I asked again, this time slower, like she hadn't heard me the first time.

She held her ground and gave me that stare again. "I think you know exactly what I'm talking about, Leon."

"Oh my goodness. Are you back to that again?"

She nodded.

"I told you it's not true. I was just messing around when I told you all that stuff."

"And I told you that I know you're lying. Look, it's vital to your recovery that I know everything about you. I can't help you if I don't fully understand all your problems."

"So you say. Can we change the subject, please?"

She hesitated for a second, then pushed aside her notebook and removed her glasses. "Sure. There's something else I need to talk to you about anyway."

"What?" I snapped. I was starting to feel like this woman was just inventing stuff about me to keep me coming back for more therapy.

"Someone broke into my office this weekend."

I raised an eyebrow. "So what does that have to do with me? I didn't do it."

"I believe you, but the police may want to talk to you about it."

"For what?"

Roberta let out a deep sigh. "Unfortunately, your file was one of the ones taken from my file cabinet."

"My file? I thought doctors kept stuff on computers nowadays."

"My computer records contain your insurance information, billing, and stuff like that, but the notes that I write during our sessions are kept in my file cabinet."

My eyes swiftly landed on her notebook, that damn pad where she was constantly scribbling down everything I said—and who knows what else. Maybe that's how she stopped herself from sharing her personal opinions; she wrote them all in those notes.

I leaned forward and narrowed my eyes at her. "What exactly did you have in my files?"

She tried to be subtle about it, but I saw her roll her chair backward a few inches as if she felt the need to put some distance between us. "I had some recordings of your hypnosis sessions and my notes from your sessions." She said it nonchalantly, like she hadn't just told me that some total stranger now had access to every humiliating detail of my life that Roberta had managed to unearth during our sessions.

"You're joking, right?" I shouted as I stood up from my seat. She scooted back another foot, this time not trying to hide the movement. "Don't you keep that shit under lock and key?"

"Yes, I do. Whoever it was broke the lock." She was still talking in that calm, rhythmic voice that they probably practice in therapist school or whatever. I used to find it soothing, but now it was just pissing me off that she didn't seem to understand how bad this was.

"Roberta, what *exactly* did you have in your notes?"

"Everything. Everything we ever talked about."

My mind raced back to the start of my therapy sessions, then did a quick fast-forward as I remembered some of our more intense sessions. Holy shit. Twice a week for practically a year. That was a whole lot of "everything" I'd shared, all compiled into one very embarrassing file. That folder was full of my confidential information, some of which I hadn't even shared with Loraine, and now it was out there somewhere.

"You mean to tell me that somebody's out there with all my personal shit?" My heart was in my stomach. "This is bullshit. If that file gets in the wrong hands—"

"I know it doesn't help, but I'm sorry."

"Sorry? What the hell is it with you, woman? Sorry isn't good enough."

In a sudden burst of rage, I swiped my arm across Roberta's desk, knocking her notebook, lamp, and telephone to the floor. She screamed and jumped up from her chair. It gave me an odd sense of satisfaction to see her finally show some damn emotion. With that, I stormed out of the office, wondering if things could possibly get any worse for me.

Loraine

23

I was weaving in and out of traffic on I-64 like a bat out of hell, trying to get home from work before Leon's imposed 6:30 PM curfew. Usually I was home by six o'clock with time to spare, but today, my late-afternoon conference call went longer than expected, and I didn't get to leave the building until 5:30. I tried to call Leon and let him know I might be late, but he didn't answer his phone. Not that it would have mattered. I'm sure he would have flipped out on me, accusing me of meeting up with Michael somewhere, or screaming his usual insult: *If you'd kept your damn legs closed, you wouldn't have a damn curfew.*

As I picked up my speed, my cell phone started ringing. I halfway expected it to be Leon, but I wasn't surprised when I saw Michael's number on the caller ID. This was his twentieth call today. He sure as hell wasn't making this easy. I would have loved to know who gave him my new number so I could strangle that person. There was a chance it was this guy Herman we both know, but since I had no proof, all I could do was hit IGNORE for the millionth time.

I had to fight the urge to answer the phone, though. As much as I wanted to speak to Michael, I didn't dare. Leon had all our phone accounts on lockdown. He checked the online statements and the voice messages practically every half hour to see who I called and who called me. He even had all my text messages, business and personal, forwarded to his cell phone. Every ounce of my independent spirit wanted to protest his jail warden's mentality, but I knew that the second I did, we would be headed to divorce court, and I wasn't ready for that.

"Michael, please stop calling, baby. It's nothing I can do," I said aloud, as if he could hear me.

By the time I parked in my driveway, it was 6:39 and I was nine minutes late. Dammit, I did not want to hear his mouth. He had me on such a short leash these days that even when I did make it home on time, I had to report to him every detail of my day, at which point I never knew what would set him off.

It was what his therapist called "transparency," where I had to disclose all my activities until Leon regained his trust in our marriage. I'd had to stop using Facebook, Twitter, and MySpace. So far, I'd been good; however, this whole situation was starting to get old quick—not to mention the fact that I missed the hell out of Michael.

I sat in the car for a few minutes, enjoying my last few minutes of peace before I had to deal with Leon's bull. Maybe I could shut him up with a quickie. Then again, everything was quick with him. But he did love a good blow job. Yeah, that's what I would do to avoid a fight.

"Leon, baby, I've got a surprise for you," I called out when I went into the house. I was surprised he wasn't standing there waiting to go off on me for missing curfew. I called his name again and still got no answer. He was home; that much I did know, because his truck was in the driveway.

As unlikely as it was, maybe he was taking a nap. Wouldn't that be something? I could sneak into the room and turn the clock back fifteen minutes before I woke him up, and then all would be well in the Farrow household.

I decided that wasn't such a bad plan, so I tiptoed quietly up the stairs.

When I opened the door, hoping I'd find him asleep in the bed, it took my brain a few seconds to process what I actually saw. Leon was lying on the floor, but his body was twisted in a strange position, not his usual fetal-position rest. *Jesus Christ, he's had a heart attack,* was the first coherent thought I was able to put together, but when I rushed to him and tried to move him, I discovered how wrong I was. I put my hand on his midsection to turn him over and felt something slippery and wet. I pulled back and looked down to see my palm covered with blood.

Again, there was that strange moment in time between my eyes taking in the sight and my brain finally figuring out what it meant. And once I knew that it was my husband's blood I was looking at, my terrified screams shattered the silence.

I barely remember what happened after that moment. The only reason I can say I called 911 is because I heard the tape of the call later. Even as anguished as my voice sounded during that frantic call, I had no way of knowing then that this horrific moment was only the beginning of more pain to come.

Jerome

24

I walked through the door carrying two bags of groceries, smiling from ear to ear. There was nothing like coming home to a clean house, and mine was so clean I could still smell the Pine-Sol. I'd hired this Latino couple, Roxanna and Carlos, after Egypt recommended them, and they did the damn thing. That woman had her husband moving furniture, going up on ladders to clean my ceiling fans . . . all kinds of work I would have never done myself. I don't think my house had even been this clean when I bought the place brand-new.

Now all I had to do was cook, and, boy, did I have one hell of a meal planned. The main course would be bourbon brine–roasted turkey legs with honey barbecue sauce, a recipe I'd gotten out of *Essence* magazine. Side dishes of collard greens and glazed autumn root vegetables would complete the feast. Once I finished preparing the meal and setting the table, I would lower the lamps and light vanilla-scented candles throughout the room.

I used to cook like this at least once a month. I'd prepare all of Big Poppa's favorites and then present them on a perfectly decorated, candlelit table. I was like Martha Stewart in the body of a gay black man. It was my way of showing Big Poppa how much he meant to me. After a while, though, I started doing it less often. His reaction was never as grateful as I'd imagined it should be, and I started feeling taken for granted. If he was getting this type of service in my house, there would never be a reason for him to take me out to a nice, romantic restaurant. I was making it too easy for him to keep me in the compartment he seemed to want me in: occasional fuck buddy, definitely not someone he'd proudly take out in public.

I shook my head as if it would erase the unhappy memories I was focusing on. I had more important things to do, like prepare this fabulous meal for my friend Hannah and the special guest she was bringing. Hannah was a friend I knew from my old job. We weren't best friends by any means, but after everything that had happened, I needed someone to talk to. Even more so, I needed someone who could make me laugh, and Hannah used to be able to do that when we occasionally hung out at a happy hour after work. So, I called her and asked her to meet me at a local bar.

It was good to see her and talk about old times—happier times. We stayed away from difficult subjects, especially her boss, who happened to be my ex–best friend Loraine. I still missed her terribly. Hannah didn't know the details behind why Loraine fired me, but she knew enough not to bring her up now. I also didn't tell her about Ron's death. Like Big Poppa, she might have read about it in the papers, but if she did, she was classy enough not to mention it.

I did, however, share with her the news that I had finally broken up with Big Poppa. He was still calling me on the regular, telling me how much he loved me, but I'd stood my ground. I missed the hell out of him, but I made it clear that we were never getting back together as long as he was still with his wife.

Hannah tried to hide a smile when I told her, but I knew she wasn't sorry about the breakup. She didn't necessarily have a problem with me being gay, but she definitely didn't like that I was sleeping with married men. Once she heard that Big Poppa was no longer in the picture, she started jabbering away about this friend she wanted me to meet. His name was Jake, and from her description, he sounded like my physical type. The one thing about him that would be new and different for me? He was a gay man who was out of the closet.

Somehow, the timing seemed right. For the longest time, I had only liked men who were in the closet, especially married men. I don't know; I guess it was the whole "thrill of the chase" thing, like it proved I was the bomb if I could turn out all these supposedly straight dudes. A shrink would have a field day with me, no doubt.

Now I was realizing that my thing for straight guys was more than just a game; it had hurt a lot of people. Freddie got his ass kicked by his wife because of it. Big Poppa was living in this kind of limbo, and he never really seemed happy with who he was. Peter had gone off the deep end and turned into a psycho stalker. And of course there was Ron, who had paid the ultimate price. Yeah, maybe it was time to give openly gay men a try.

While the turkey was in the oven, I went to my bedroom to put on my best suit. I sure hoped this guy Jake was worth all the effort I was making.

My phone rang, and I smiled when I looked down and saw Egypt's number on the caller ID. She worked with Hannah, so no doubt the two of them had been gossiping all day about my blind date. Egypt was probably calling to tease me.

"Hey, girl," I said when I answered the call. "Those cleaning people you recommended were incredible."

"Jerome," she said in a voice that was definitely not light-hearted. "You need to get down to MCV right now."

"MCV? As in the hospital? For what?"

"Loraine needs you."

I swear to God it felt like my heart screeched to a halt. "Oh my God. Is she all right?" We hadn't spoken in such a long time, but I still had much love for Loraine, and I always would.

"It's not Loraine; it's her husband. He's been shot."

I almost dropped the phone. "Leon got shot?"

"Three times in the chest."

"You lying. That shit ain't funny, Egypt." Maybe that sounds like a strange thing for me to say, but if you knew Egypt, you'd understand. When Loraine and I first had our falling out, Egypt had tried everything she knew to get us back together. Now, because I didn't want to believe yet another tragedy had occurred, I convinced myself this was just another ploy to get me to call Loraine.

"I wouldn't lie about something like this, Jerome. You need to get down here. Loraine needs you. She needs all the real friends she can get. I know y'all ain't been speaking since she fired you, but a real friend is always there in a time of need—no matter what."

"I'll be there in twenty minutes," I said before disconnecting the call.

I found Egypt and Loraine sitting in the surgical waiting room at MCV. Loraine looked like hell. Her eyes were red and puffy, and black trails of mascara ran down her cheeks. She stood up when she saw me approaching, and I grabbed her and hugged her with all my strength. It was as if all the drama between us had never happened. She had been my best friend for years, and no matter what we had been through, it felt so right to have my arms around her.

"I'm sorry, girl. I'm so sorry," I said. These are the same words most people speak when comforting someone during a tragedy, but for me, there were so many layers of meaning. Maybe someday we would repair our friendship and I could truly apologize for everything; but for now, we could deal with only the awful situation at hand. "Is Leon all right?"

"He's in surgery."

I could see the tears glistening in her eyes, and that just made my eyes begin to water. We stared at each other for a moment. I was left speechless by the surreal situation, not only because her husband had been shot, but also because I was standing in front of the friend I thought I had lost forever.

"They shot him, Jerome. They shot my husband." I pulled her into another tight embrace and held her as she cried. "I can't believe they shot my husband."

I kept my arms around Loraine but turned my attention to Egypt to try to get a grasp of the situation. "What happened?"

"I don't really know," Egypt answered. "Loraine told me that she came home and found him on the bedroom floor. The police are over there now trying to gather evidence."

"There was so much blood," Loraine sobbed.

I felt my body tensing with anger. I hoped like hell that the police would find whoever did this in a hurry, and make them pay.

Loraine

25

We'd been sitting in the waiting room for several long, tense hours while doctors worked to remove the bullets from Leon's body and repair the internal damage. I still felt numb, not able to put all the pieces together in my mind. From the ambulance ride to the emergency room to hearing the doctors say Leon would die without surgery, it all felt so surreal. I don't know what I would have done without the support of my good friends by my side.

When Egypt told me she had called Jerome, I didn't protest for the first time in a long time. In the midst of this nightmare, everything Jerome had done in the past seemed minor. This was life or death, and I couldn't think of anyone I wanted by my side to get me through this more than Jerome.

He was my first real friend. At one time, he was the person who understood me best, the person I could share everything with. When he wrapped his arms around me, it reassured me in a way I can't even really explain. Egypt had been a wonderful friend and a strong supporter, and I loved her for it, but it just wasn't the same. Something about the way Jerome held me let me know that he was feeling my pain as if it were his own.

"It's going to be all right," Jerome said with a sigh, stroking my arm absentmindedly and staring off into space.

I put my head on his shoulder. "Thanks for being here for me." I wiped away a tear that had escaped and was making its way down my cheek. "I know you've never really liked Leon, so it means a lot that you're here praying for him now."

He turned and looked into my eyes. "Loraine, I—"

"Mrs. Farrow?" I looked up and saw two black men approaching us. My heart skipped a beat in fear that they were here to deliver bad news, but then I realized they were wearing suits, not scrubs, so they weren't doctors.

The lighter-skinned man spoke. "I'm Detective Tyndale. This is my partner, Detective Ryan. We're investigating your husband's shooting, and we'd like to ask you a few questions, if you don't mind."

I lifted my head off of Jerome's shoulder. He squeezed my hand to remind me he would be by my side through this. "Okay."

"We just came from your house. It appears someone broke into your home through the rear bathroom window."

"A burglar?" I asked.

"I really doubt it. I know you haven't had a chance to do an inventory, but nothing seemed out of place. You had diamonds on your dresser, your husband had a Rolex and his wallet on the nightstand. Plus there are three plasma TVs in the house. I don't think it was a robbery."

"You mean to tell us somebody shot him deliberately?" Jerome bolted out of his chair angrily, but the other officer gave him a stare that sent him right back to his seat.

Detective Tyndale ignored Jerome and remained calm. "We're not ruling it out. Mrs. Farrow, does your husband have any enemies?"

My hand flew to my mouth. Why hadn't any of this entered my mind until now? Probably because I didn't want to face it. I had a sudden flashback of the threat Michael had made at the hotel when we first got back together. He'd told me that if I dumped him again, he wouldn't be responsible for his actions. Then when Leon pulled up next to us in his car, Michael pulled out a gun. And finally, when he showed up at the house, he'd threatened Leon's life. I'd never believed Michael had it in him to act on his threats, but now that Leon was fighting for his life, I couldn't be sure.

"He wouldn't do something like this. He's not that kind of person," I mumbled.

"Who?" Jerome asked before the detective could even speak.

I looked at him and opened my mouth, but no words would come out.

"We really need to know who you're talking about, Mrs. Farrow," Detective Ryan said.

I wanted to disappear so I wouldn't have to face any of this. My husband was lying in a hospital bed, and there was a possibility that I had something to do with it. The full weight of my affair suddenly became clear to me. I thought I was just fulfilling my sexual needs, but now I saw that nothing was ever that simple. My selfish desires led to serious consequences in other people's lives too. I felt guilty and ashamed, and the last thing I wanted to do was admit I was an adulteress, but I had to tell the truth. If there was the slightest possibility Michael had done this, I wanted him buried under the jail.

"The only enemy Leon has is Michael, the man I've been seeing," I answered, barely above a whisper.

"Huh?" Jerome gasped. "I thought he was out of the picture." When I wouldn't look at him or answer, Jerome turned to Egypt. "She's still messing with Michael?"

Egypt placed her index finger to her lips and gave him a harsh look. "Shush! It's a long story, and now is not the time to be talking about it."

"Did you say this Michael is your boyfriend?" Detective Ryan asked, and I thought I heard judgment in his tone.

I couldn't bring myself to answer him. I felt humiliated.

"Mrs. Farrow, this is something we need to know," he pushed. "Any information you can share might help to catch your husband's attacker."

At the mention of my husband, I snapped out of my self-absorbed embarrassment. This wasn't about me; it was about justice for Leon.

"He's the man I was having an affair with. He came to my house with a gun two weeks ago."

Detective Tyndale raised an eyebrow and whipped out a small pad. "We need his full name and address so we can go talk to this man."

I gave him the information, adding, "He was very upset when

we broke up, but I don't believe he has anything to do with this."

"Well, that might be the case, ma'am, but we still need to question him, even if it's just to rule him out as a suspect."

"When's the last time you saw him?" Detective Ryan asked. I gave him the answer, as well as answers to the dozens of other questions they peppered me with. By the time they were done, I felt naked, having exposed every intimate detail of my affair.

As far as having a motive for the shooting, Michael certainly looked like a prime suspect. Both Jerome and Egypt were convinced that he was guilty as sin. I couldn't condemn him that quickly, though. I wanted to hear what Michael had to say for himself. I hoped like hell that he had an airtight alibi. I was not ready to believe a man I'd been sleeping with could be so violent.

Before the detectives left, they promised to be in touch if there were any developments in the case.

I slumped back into one of the uncomfortable chairs. Jerome placed his arm around my shoulder. "Do you think Michael did it?" he asked.

I shook my head. "I don't know, but that's their job to figure it out. Right now I'm only concerned about one thing: whether Leon is going to live or die."

He wrapped me in another tight embrace. "Everything's going to be okay," he said. While his words were confident, I could feel his whole body trembling against mine.

Michael

26

It was almost nine o'clock by the time I finished painting my garage and came in the house. I was tired but feeling good. My plan to rekindle my relationship with Loraine was in full swing. If I knew her, she was probably beside herself with grief right now, and it was only a matter of time before she'd be calling me to come be by her side.

I could think of a million reasons why she should have chosen me over Leon when she was given the chance, but instead of standing up for our love, she crumpled like tissue paper when Leon threatened to divorce her. I almost felt bad for Loraine now that I'd taken matters into my own hands. Things were going to be rough on her for a while, at least until I stepped in as her white knight.

I sat down on the sofa, sipping a drink and casually thumbing through some papers in a folder on my coffee table. Every time I flipped through them, a smile crept up on my face. This whole thing had almost been too easy.

My doorbell rang, which surprised me. Was Loraine so upset that she'd come racing to my house already? I knew my plan was good, but I hadn't expected it to work this fast. I looked down at my paint-stained clothes, wishing I had time to change before she saw me, but a loud, insistent knock made me close the folder and get up from the sofa.

I cracked open the door and was more than a little disappointed to see that it wasn't Loraine standing outside. "Can I help you?" I asked the two men before me, who wore dark trench coats and very serious expressions.

"Michael Richards?"

"Yeah. Who's asking?"

They flashed badges. "My name's Detective Tyndale. This is my partner, Detective Ryan. Can we step inside?"

Holy shit. Had Loraine called the cops on me? Why would she do that? And how the hell would she even know it was me?

"Sure, sure," I said, fighting to maintain my composure. "What can I do for you? Is everything all right?" I stepped back and watched them enter my living room.

Tyndale spun around and faced me, while Ryan began wandering around the room. I wanted to ask Ryan what the hell he was looking for, but Detective Tyndale started in on me with questions, forcing my attention toward him.

"You know Loraine Farrow?" he asked.

I felt my stomach tighten in fear. So Loraine had spoken to the cops. This was not at all how I had planned for things to go down. "Yes, I know her," I said reluctantly.

"You know her husband, Leon?"

"Yeah, of course I know him. What's this all about? Is Loraine all right?" My heart started pounding and my palms were sweating. This was a possibility I never thought of: What if Loraine became so distraught about Leon that she hurt herself? "Is she all right?" I yelled.

"Yes, Mrs. Farrow is fine." Detective Tyndale's voice was abrupt and borderline nasty. "But you need to understand something. I'm asking the questions right now, okay?"

I nodded.

"Now, when was the last time you saw Leon Farrow?"

"I don't know. Why?"

"I told you I'll ask the questions."

Things were getting more uncomfortable by the second. Maybe I hadn't thought out my plan so well after all. "Well, I know my rights, and I'm not going to answer any questions until you tell me what the hell is going on."

Tyndale glanced over at his partner, who was looking through my bookcase. A smirk passed between them. Ryan said, "Well, if he doesn't know what's going on"—there was that smirk again—"then go ahead and tell him."

Tyndale looked at me again. "We're investigating a shooting. Leon Farrow has been shot and—"

"What?" In all my fantasies about how my plan would come to fruition, I certainly never dreamed this moment, standing here having a conversation like this with the cops. My head was buzzing with confusion and panic. I felt trapped, and I knew they weren't going to share any more details with me to help me figure things out.

"I said Leon Farrow has been shot. Is something wrong, Mr. Richards? Something you want to tell us?" He was eyeing me suspiciously as he said it.

I instantly went on the defensive. "Like what?"

The detective gave me a hard stare and raised his eyebrows like he was just waiting for me to fuck up and say the wrong thing so they could arrest me.

"Oh, no," I said, shaking my head. "No way. You've got this all wrong. I didn't shoot anyone. I didn't kill Leon."

Ryan approached me and stood close enough that I could feel his breath on my face. "But you've been known to threaten Leon, haven't you?" he asked.

His partner quickly added, "And you've been known to carry a gun, right?"

I looked from one to the other, wondering just how much they knew about me and the way I'd been pursuing Loraine. What had she told them about me?

"You do own a gun, don't you, Mr. Richards?" Tyndale barked at me.

There was no sense in lying about it. These guys were coming on too strong to not already know about the gun I'd purchased. "Yeah, I own a gun," I replied quietly.

"What kind of gun?" Ryan asked.

"A twenty-two-caliber automatic."

"Hmm, that's interesting. Leon Farrow was shot with a twenty-two."

I felt my knees wobbling and had to reach out and rest my hand on the couch to keep from falling. This just kept getting worse.

"Something wrong, Mr. Richards?"

"No, no, this is all just a little surprising."

Again he smirked.

"So where's your gun now, Mr. Richards?" Ryan asked.

"I threw it in the James River."

"Threw it in the James River?" Tyndale repeated mockingly. "You don't expect us to believe that, do you?"

"Look, I know how this sounds, but it's the truth."

Ryan chuckled, then started pacing around the room again. "You really must think we're stupid."

Tyndale kept pressing me. "Where were you this afternoon?"

"I was here by myself. I spent most of the afternoon painting my garage."

"Can anybody verify that?"

"No. I was here alone."

He shook his head. "Mr. Richards, I really have to tell you this doesn't look good. Maybe we should finish our questioning downtown."

"For what? I didn't shoot Leon. I didn't have to. His wife was gonna leave him today anyway."

"Oh, really?" He looked at me like he thought I was delusional. "That's not what she told us."

"Leon Farrow," Detective Ryan said from across the room.

I looked in his direction and saw that he was holding the folder I'd left on my coffee table. As he opened it and read silently for a few seconds, I tried to imagine how things would play out if I tried to run.

" 'Dr. Roberta Marshall, psychiatrist,' " he read out loud, then looked up at me. "What are you doing with this file? This looks to me like you're in possession of some confidential medical files. Care to explain?"

I started sputtering. "I . . . I . . ." Shit, now I was really in trouble. "Um, maybe I need to talk to a lawyer before I answer that."

"Yeah, maybe you do." Detective Tyndale pulled out a pair of handcuffs. "Turn around and put your hands behind your back. You're under arrest for the attempted murder of Leon Farrow."

Loraine

27

Leon made it through surgery and had been moved to the intensive care unit. We were in the corridor outside his room, waiting for the doctors to finish checking him before they would allow us in. As we watched through the glass, I couldn't get over the number of tubes and wires trailing to his body from the IV bags and machines surrounding his bed. He'd survived the surgery, but he definitely didn't look good. All they'd told me so far was that he wasn't out of the woods yet. I was hoping the doctor would give me something a little more concrete when he finished his examination. Up until now, I'd tried to be optimistic, but after seeing Leon, I was starting to prepare myself for the worst.

I leaned against Jerome for support as I watched the doctors work on Leon, and imagined my life without him. Thank God I'd had my friends by my side throughout the night. Egypt had finally gone home around midnight to be with her husband and baby, but she was still constantly texting words of encouragement and checking in for updates. Jerome hadn't left me alone, and I was so grateful, because without him there, I would have spent the night beating myself up. It was my own selfish choice, the choice to be with Michael, that led to this whole tragic nightmare.

The doctors and nurses left Leon's bedside and started coming out of the room. My back stiffened and I started wringing my hands as I waited nervously for their prognosis.

The head doctor held out his hand, and as I shook it, he introduced himself and his team.

"I'm a friend of the family." Jerome stepped in when he saw I was having trouble speaking. "How is he, Doctor?"

The doctor looked at me as if asking permission to share Leon's medical information. I nodded. "Well," he started, "I'm not going to sugarcoat it for you. Your husband's condition is very critical. As you know, we removed three bullets from his chest. Two of those bullets were lodged in his lungs; the other barely missed his heart and a main artery. We lost him and brought him back a couple of times on the operating table. Right now we've got him on a respirator, but it's still going to be an uphill battle. He lost a lot of blood."

I felt the remaining strength leave my body. Jerome wrapped his arm around me in an effort to prop me up. He asked the question I had in my mind but was unable to voice. "Is he going to make it?"

"Well, that depends. If he gets through the next twenty-four hours, then his chances will be better, but it's going to be a very long recovery. We can most likely keep him alive with a respirator."

"Thank you, Jesus," Jerome cried out. I let out a sigh, but I couldn't share Jerome's elation. I knew how Leon would have felt about the doctor's news.

"He wouldn't want to be kept alive on a respirator."

The doctors looked at me when I made my announcement.

"He signed an advance directive a few years ago when he came in here for some minor surgery. We both have them on file. Neither one of us wanted to be kept alive by artificial means. He said if it ever came to that, he'd want them to pull the plug." Tears were streaming down my face as I said this. When we signed those papers, it had felt like a formality, just something they'd asked us to do in admitting before a minor surgery with minimal risks. I'd almost forgotten the directive existed, yet now I was faced with the reality that Leon's signature on that paper might mean death.

"You sure you want to do that, Loraine?" Jerome asked with an urgency to his voice.

"Well, unfortunately it might not be a question of what she

wants, sir. If a patient has signed an advance directive, we are bound by law to honor his wishes."

"But what if he changed his mind since then? She said he signed the papers a few years ago," Jerome argued.

It was clear that things were about to get tense. The doctor defused the situation by saying, "Well, this isn't a discussion we need to have just yet anyway. It's too soon after the surgery. We need to give him some time to heal, and then we'll do a brain scan before we make any decisions or turn anything off."

"Why a brain scan?" Jerome asked. "You said he got shot in his lungs."

"He did, but we need to get an idea of his brain function; then we'll be better able to predict his chances of surviving without the respirator."

"So you mean he might not die when you take the breathing tube out?" Jerome asked hopefully.

"No, he might not, but he's lost a lot of blood, so even if he does survive, it's likely he won't ever be the same person."

"What do you mean?" Jerome snapped. "You trying to say he's gonna be a vegetable?"

"It's quite possible," the doctor answered, and I couldn't take any more.

"Can we talk about this later?" My voice cracked. Tears welled up in my eyes once again, and I was finding it hard to breathe. "I can't deal with this right now."

"Sure. Take some time to think about everything we've talked about. We'll go check his records for that advance directive. We'll come back and check on him in the next hour or two."

The second they were gone, I turned to Jerome and burst into tears. "This is all my fault! I might as well have pulled the trigger myself. If I had just left Michael alone . . . I'm not staying here if he dies. I'm gonna go be with him."

Jerome grabbed me and held me tightly in his arms. I could feel his tears soaking my shoulder. "Shhh. You're not going any-where," he murmured. "Everything's going to be okay."

We stayed like that for quite some time, with Jerome's arms wrapped around me protectively. He alternated between crying with me and comforting me.

"Mrs. Farrow?" Detective Tyndale approached us. I sat up and wiped the tears from my face.

"How's your husband?" he asked respectfully.

"He's holding on, but the doctors say he still might not make it."

"I'm really sorry to hear that. I just came by to share some news about the case."

As much as I didn't want it to be true, what he told me next was what I'd already been expecting to hear.

"We found some evidence at Michael Richards's house that links him to the crime. We arrested him last night."

If my stomach hadn't been empty, I would have regurgitated on the spot. There was no more denying it. I had cheated on my husband with a man who had ultimately tried to kill him. How could I have misjudged Michael so completely?

I wiped the tears from my eyes. "I'm prepared to give you whatever information you need to make sure that man is locked up for the rest of his life. He's taken everything from me."

In a cruel irony, Jerome's cell phone started playing the song "Secret Lovers," not exactly the song I needed to hear as I learned that my lover had indeed shot my husband. He pulled the phone out of his pocket and quickly silenced it, looking quite flustered.

"Excuse me while I answer this," he said, and rushed away from us.

"Mrs. Farrow," Detective Tyndale said, "you don't have to worry about anything. We have a mountain of evidence against Michael Richards. There's no way that guy is ever going to spend another day as a free man. Matter of fact, my partner and the assistant commonwealth attorney are making that very clear to him as we speak."

It was little consolation. No amount of jail time would turn back the hands of time and make my husband whole again. I covered my face with my hands and wept. "This is all my fault. If I had kept my damn legs closed, none of this would have happened."

Michael

28

"Well, Bill, your client's in a lot of trouble." Maria Russo, an attorney for the commonwealth, smirked confidently as she sat back in her chair. She was sitting next to Detective Ryan, across the table from my attorney, Bill Thorn, and me. We were in the Richmond Police Department's interrogation room, and to be quite honest, I was scared to death. They'd charged me with attempted murder. Although the evidence was piling up against me, and I'd thought about killing Leon plenty of times, this was a crime I didn't commit. Sure, I'd done some really messed up shit in the past few days in the name of love, including breaking into Leon's shrink's office, but I didn't do this. I didn't shoot the man.

The only person who seemed to believe me was my lawyer, and I'd only been able to speak to him briefly before these two walked in.

My friend Gordon had hired Bill for me, because he was supposed to be one of the best and most connected criminal defense attorneys in Richmond. He'd earned his $10,000 retainer so far; I'd never heard of anyone else getting a commonwealth attorney to give up a Saturday morning to meet with an attorney and his client. He was a confident son of a gun too. He didn't have time to explain how, but before the two of them came into the room, he promised me he'd have the charges dropped by the end of the day. I didn't know how the hell he was going to do that with all the evidence they had on me. I just hoped he was as good as he claimed to be.

Russo said, "From what I'm hearing, it doesn't look like Leon

Farrow is going to make it through the weekend, and that changes everything from attempted murder to homicide."

"But I didn't shoot him!" I was desperate to proclaim my innocence, but Bill raised his hand and I shut up quickly. He'd made it very clear he didn't want me saying a thing unless he gave the word. That was easier said than done; it was my life on the line.

"My client's innocent, Maria," Bill replied confidently in his Southern drawl. It was obvious the two of them had bumped heads before, and she didn't like him at all.

"Yeah. So he says . . ." Her sarcasm made Detective Ryan laugh. "I guess you and your client have forgotten about the mountain of evidence we have against him. You're not going to be marching this one out of here like you did the last time, Bill."

My patience was wearing thin. I hadn't slept since I was arrested some time yesterday evening. I wanted to tell that smug bitch to kiss my ass, but my lawyer was obviously not intimidated by her, so I kept my mouth shut and let him do his job.

My lawyer countered with, "You call that evidence? It's all circumstantial at best." He chuckled, shaking his head. "Maria, you got no case."

She ticked off the list of evidence she felt did make her case. "Your client's having an affair with the victim's wife. He's threatened the victim on numerous occasions. Let's not mention the fact that he stalked Mr. Farrow and broke into his psychiatrist's office and stole his file. I think that gives me motive. Plus, Leon Farrow was shot with a twenty-two-caliber handgun, which your client just happens to own—and conveniently threw in the James River."

Bill was about to say something, but she cut him off. "Oh, did I forget to mention he has no alibi? I'm sure I can convince a jury that this was a crime of passion. So, yeah, I've got a case, a damn good one."

Bill clapped his hands a few times as if he were applauding halfheartedly. "Maria, that's a great story. I'm surprised you haven't gone to the press with it already."

"Only reason I haven't is because Saturdays are such slow news days. But that won't be the case after his arraignment

Monday morning—that is, unless you and your client are willing to take a plea and save the commonwealth a trial. How's twenty-to-life sound? He'll still have a chance at parole."

I looked at my lawyer in a panic. "I'm not taking twenty-to-life. I didn't do this. I didn't shoot that man."

Bill raised his hand again. I shut up, but he was starting to piss me off. Who the hell did he think he was, Perry Mason? This lady meant business, and he seemed more interested in antagonizing her than defending me. I didn't really give a shit what their personal feud was all about. Didn't he realize my life was on the line?

My lawyer continued with his sarcastic approach. "From where I'm sitting, the only thing you've got on him is misdemeanor possession of stolen property. Why don't we just write him a desk appearance ticket and all go home and enjoy the weekend?"

"Are you out of your fucking mind?" Ryan finally spoke up. "This son of a bitch shot that man three times in the chest so that he could have his wife. This is an open and shut case of premeditated murder!"

I couldn't take it anymore. I spoke up in my own defense, and this time, I didn't give a shit if my lawyer tried to stop me. "I didn't have to shoot him! She was going to leave him on her own."

"Really? That's not what she told my partner," Ryan snapped. "She told him she tried to break it off with you but you kept calling her."

"Hold on a minute." My lawyer interrupted, probably to stop this little confrontation between me and Ryan before I admitted to something I shouldn't, like the fact that I had been ringing her phone off the hook and I did break into that doctor's office. "Let me get something straight: Your motive is that my client wanted Mr. Farrow dead so that he could have his wife?"

"Damn right," Ryan answered, slamming his hand down on the table. He'd already convicted me.

Bill sat back in his chair and folded his arms across his chest. "Have either of you looked in that file?"

A sideways glance passed between Ryan and Russo. Obviously neither of them had bothered to read it. She admitted,

"No. It has no bearing on this case other than to prove your client's obsession with both Mr. and Mrs. Farrow."

"Oh, I'm not so sure of that," Bill countered, oozing arrogance. "Michael, why don't you tell them why you feel so strongly that Mrs. Farrow was going to leave her husband."

Finally, it was my chance to explain. "I mailed a copy of the file to Loraine. I even highlighted the important parts for her. I knew that once she read them, there was no way she would stay with Leon."

"So what?" Ryan jumped in before I could finish. "That doesn't prove a damn thing," he said.

My lawyer leaned forward. "Actually, I think it does. You see, the pages my client highlighted contained notes concerning your victim's sexuality."

"I still fail to see the relevance," Ms. Russo said, but her posture suggested that her confidence was wavering, like she knew how Bill Thorn operated and that he was about to blow holes in their theory.

"Mr. Farrow is homosexual. Or bisexual, if you want to be politically correct. He'd been having a gay affair for years. My client had no reason to resort to violence. He knew that mailing the file would be enough to break up their already-shaky marriage. If you'd read the file, you'd know that Mr. Farrow has some performance issues in the bedroom with Mrs. Farrow."

"Shit. She didn't tell us about any of that." Ryan opened the folder and started flipping pages. When he reached the highlighted material, he dropped his head in his hands. I guess he'd expected this case to be open and shut.

Bill couldn't resist getting in another shot at Ms. Russo. "Tell me something, Maria." He looked down at her ring finger. "You're married. What would you do if you found out your husband was sleeping with another guy? Especially if, as my client tells me, the guy he was sleeping with had been *your* best friend? Perhaps we should start looking at the wife or perhaps even the gay lover. They both certainly have motive, don't you think?"

Ryan groaned and closed the folder. I wanted to laugh at him. He was no longer the same cocky son of a bitch who'd strolled around my house yesterday like he owned the place. I hoped his sergeant ripped him and his partner a new asshole for this fuckup.

Ms. Russo wasn't ready to accept defeat. "There's still the question of that weapon."

"Which you don't have," Bill reminded her.

"Because your client threw it in the river," she countered. "Who throws away a brand-new gun unless you have something to hide? A jury might find that to be very suspicious behavior."

"You're a little too confident for your own good sometimes, you know that, Maria?"

I couldn't believe what I was seeing. These two were having a pissing match, trying to prove who was the better lawyer. I don't think it mattered to them whether I was innocent; they were only interested in winning this competition they seemed to have going on between them.

"Hah! I'm too confident? At least I'm not delusional. Why don't you just give it up and explain to your client that you're out of your league and he should find better representation? I still have him dead to rights."

Bill smiled at her. "On the contrary. He's already hired the best in town." He reached into his briefcase and pulled out a DVD, which he slid across the table to her.

"What's this?" she asked.

"You said the crime occurred sometime between four-thirty and six, correct?"

"Yes."

"Good, then you can release my client now."

Russo laughed out loud. "There's that good old Bill Thorn arrogance again. And why, exactly, should I release him?"

"That DVD was taken from the security camera outside Mr. Richards's neighbor's home. From the neighbor's backyard surveillance camera, you'll see there's a clear view of a portion of Mr. Richards's property."

"And?" Ms. Russo tried to look unimpressed, but I could tell she was feeling her case fall apart before her eyes.

"And Mr. Richards can be seen painting his garage during the hours that the crime took place." He looked over at Detective Ryan. "Did you and your partner happen to notice that my client was covered in paint when you arrested him?"

Ryan couldn't even make eye contact with my lawyer when he mumbled, "No."

We didn't exactly live in a bad neighborhood, so I'd always thought John Simpkins was paranoid for having those cameras installed. Now I made a mental note to bring him a bottle of Scotch and thank him for his help.

Ms. Russo sighed like she finally knew the fight between her and Bill Thorn had been won, and not by her.

Bill delivered the final nail to the coffin. "And just so you don't waste everyone's time trying to question the authenticity of this disk, I have a sworn affidavit from John Reynolds, who re-trieved the security footage from Mr. Simpkins's home late last night." He turned to Ryan again. "You might have known him as *Captain* John Reynolds before he retired from the force. He works as an investigator for my firm now."

Detective Ryan turned to look at Russo and said, "Reynolds is as straight as an arrow. There's no way that DVD is a fake."

Russo threw her pen down on her legal pad. She looked like she wanted to punch Ryan in the face.

"Well," Bill said happily, "I think we can all agree that my client couldn't have been in two places at one time, so there goes your case." He made a big show of checking his watch and giv-ing a leisurely stretch, like beating Russo was all in a day's work for him.

He turned and patted me on the back. "You know, Michael, we'll have you out of here so soon that I might still be able to fit in a round of golf today."

Jerome

29

I walked away from Loraine and the detective in a hurry, heading around a corner and down a deserted hallway where no nurses would tell me to turn off my cell phone. I wanted to stay and hear what evidence they had against this guy Michael, but Big Poppa's ring tone threw me for a loop.

My hands were shaking when I answered the call.

"Hello?"

"Hey there, Lover Boy."

The voice sent chills down my spine. It was Peter.

"Didn't I tell you I'd find out who Big Poppa was?"

It took me a minute to gather my senses and ask, "How the fuck did you get his phone?" He had me so shook that my voice came out sounding breathless and weak.

Peter laughed wickedly. "That's for me to know and you to find out. I'll be in touch."

He disconnected the call, and I stood there flabbergasted, staring at the phone. For a second, I tried to convince myself that maybe I hadn't heard Big Poppa's ring tone after all. Maybe Peter was calling me from some other number. But Peter's words still rang in my ears—*Didn't I tell you I'd find out who Big Poppa was?*—and I knew that this was more than a bad dream. This was really happening. Peter was truly in possession of Big Poppa's phone, and in my bewildered state, I didn't yet grasp all the ramifications of what that meant.

I headed back down the hall toward the ICU. What was I going to do about that call? For a second I thought about getting in my car to find Peter and strangling him with my bare hands. But it wouldn't do any good. That motherfucker was probably long gone by now.

Maybe I could pull the detective aside and talk to him about Peter, but he was too amped up about this guy Michael now, and it was too late anyway. When I arrived, Tyndale was already gone, and Loraine was in Leon's room, crying beside his bed.

I pulled up a chair and sat next to her. "You all right?"

She wiped her tears, then turned to me, releasing a long sigh. "I'm gonna go take a walk. I've got to get some air."

"You want me to go with you?"

"No, I think I need a little time alone."

"I know that's right. I'm feeling pretty tense myself. You go ahead. We'll talk when you come back."

I watched her leave the room, then spent a few minutes just staring at Leon. The *whoosh* of the ventilator pumping air into his lungs competed with the beeping of all the monitors he was hooked up to. I followed one set of wires that went from his chest up to a computer screen above his bed. This was the monitor that mattered the most. It measured the beating of Leon's heart. As long as that kept pumping, he was still with us.

"I know you think I hate you," I said when I finally found the strength to speak to his motionless body. "But I don't hate you, man. I never have."

The machines droned on, but of course there was no response from Leon. I kept talking, because there was always the chance that he could hear me. Even if he couldn't, I felt the need to unburden myself of all the things that weighed so heavily on my soul right now.

"Man, I really want you to pull through this. You know you've been pretty lucky so far. You've beat the odds and made it through the night. Now all you got to do is prove these doctors wrong."

I wiped away my tears. "I will make you this one promise,

though, because I know in your heart you really love Loraine. In spite of everything, I know you've always loved her.

"No matter what happens, you don't have to worry about her. I will take care of her for you. And if by chance another man comes into her life, I'll make it my personal responsibility to make sure he does her no harm."

Loraine

30

I could hardly put one foot in front of the other as I headed for the elevator. I needed to get the hell out of that intensive care unit before I lost my mind. Ever since the doctor told me how bad it was looking for Leon, I felt like I was holding on to my sanity by a thread. How in the world was I supposed to deal with the possibility that they might pull the plug and Leon would be gone? And if he did survive, was I really prepared for the round-the-clock care he would need? The worst part of all was the realization that Michael was the shooter—Michael, who never would have done this if I hadn't invited him back into my life. Why hadn't I left him alone? More importantly, why hadn't I taken his stalking more seriously? I should have known he could become dangerous.

I was exhausted, both physically and mentally. I paced outside the hospital entrance for a while, hoping the fresh air would clear my mind, but it did no good. Maybe some caffeine would help. Even an artificial boost would be welcome right now.

I headed back inside to find the cafeteria but remembered that I'd left my wallet upstairs. Reluctantly, I got back on the elevator, feeling no better than before. Little did I know, I was about to feel even worse.

I saw Jerome sitting in a chair next to the bed, talking to Leon. It actually warmed my heart to see it, because the two of them had never really gotten along in the past. Leon was always so darn homophobic, and Jerome knew it. Add to that all the times I'd cried on Jerome's shoulder when Leon and I fought, and it was no wonder they didn't like each other. One day I would still have to address the whole idea that Jerome had tried to make me believe Leon was cheating, but that could wait. Right now, I had to give Jerome a whole lot of credit. He looked genuinely emotional as he sat there talking to my husband in that hospital bed.

I decided to hang back in the doorway so that Jerome could make his peace with Leon.

"I will make you this one promise, though, because I know in your heart that you really love Loraine. In spite of everything, I know you've always loved her."

I was moved by his words. He sounded like he finally understood what I'd been trying to tell him all along. We'd had our share of fights, but Leon wasn't a bad man, and our marriage was meant to be.

"No matter what happens, you don't have to worry about her," Jerome continued. "I'll take care of her for you. And if by chance another man comes into the picture, I'll make it my personal responsibility to make sure he does her no harm."

I smiled. That might have been the single sweetest thing I'd ever heard. Any hard feelings that might have lingered between me and Jerome were now one hundred percent gone. I was about to walk into that room and wrap my arms around my friend, but I got only one foot inside the door before his next statement stopped me in my tracks.

"I only wish things could have been different between us."

Something about the way he said it confused me. I mean, I knew he was hurt that Leon made fun of his homosexuality, but "different between us" sounded more personal somehow. He still hadn't sensed my presence. I waited to hear what he would say next.

"I wish you could have loved me the way you loved her." I watched in shocked silence as Jerome bent down and kissed Leon's hand. "I could have been such a good man to you."

For a second I thought maybe I was misinterpreting things, but there was no other explanation. It appeared that Jerome had had feelings for my husband. This was almost too much to comprehend. My best friend had had a crush on my husband. Was that the real reason he'd tried to break us up? Maybe Leon had sensed this all along, and that's why he had such a problem with Jerome.

"I still can't believe what the doctors are saying. You have to get through this. I want to hear you tell me again that you love me."

What the . . . ? I have to be hallucinating, I thought.

But no, it was real. It was slowly dawning on me that this was much deeper than just some crush he had on Leon. This was something the two of them shared, and what Jerome said next confirmed it in the worst possible way.

"I know I should have reciprocated and told you how much I loved you the last time you were at the house, and I'm sorry." He wiped away tears. "But I'll always have my memories, and you will always be my Big Poppa. I love you, Leon. I'll never forget the time we spent together."

"You motherfucker!" I screamed as I pounced on Jerome's back, punching his head and shoulders.

"Oh, shit!" He managed to shove me off long enough to get out of the chair and away from Leon's bed.

"How could you?" I cried, chasing him into a corner of the room.

"What are you talking about?" He shrugged his shoulders like he hadn't just been busted. Little did he know I'd tried that same shit two weeks ago on Leon. It didn't work then, and it damn sure wasn't working now. "I heard everything you said, you bastard. So don't even try to lie, because I know what the fuck I heard."

He just stood there with a blank expression I wanted to slap right off his face. All the pain and suffering I'd been through— the fights with Leon, the time we broke up, even the fact that I'd started my ill-fated affair with Michael—it could all be traced back to one source. Jerome was to blame for all of it.

"Now I know why you never told me who Big Poppa was," I said wryly, "and why you tried so hard to break Leon and me up. All the time I thought you cared about me, but I was just in the way, wasn't I?"

"No, Loraine, it's not like that. You're my friend. I love you."

I slapped him so hard his neck snapped backward.

"Don't you dare tell me you love me. How could you be fucking my husband if you love me?"

Jerome stood up and faced me squarely. "Don't put your hands on me again," he said. "Now, I'm sorry you had to find out this way, but I'm not going to lie about how I feel when the man I love is dying. Yes, we were together and we were in love, but not enough for him to leave you."

After so many years fighting for my marriage to survive, then trying to fight my attraction to Michael, and now feeling like I would have to fight to keep my sanity, I had no more strength left to fight with Jerome. "How long?" I asked. "How long were you two fucking behind my back?"

He stood his ground, but tears were welling up in his eyes. "Six years," he muttered.

"You fucking bastard."

"Don't act like you're all innocent in this, Loraine. Not when it's your lover, Michael, who's responsible for all this."

"Too bad he didn't finish the job!"

I glanced over at Leon, and even as he lay there wounded and helpless, all I could think of was how much I hated him at that moment. I was about two seconds away from ripping out all the tubes and knocking over all the machines he was hooked up to. Jerome must have sensed what I was thinking, because he moved between Leon and me.

A nurse walked into the room. It took her a few seconds, but she finally sensed the tension in the room and her eyes traveled between me and Jerome.

"Everything okay?" she asked warily. She had no idea how far from okay everything was.

I pointed at Jerome. "I'd like to introduce you to Leon's next of kin. He'll be making all the medical decisions for him from this point forward. My lawyers will have the papers to you Monday morning." On that note, I walked out of the room, and hopefully out of both of their lives.

I ran out of the hospital more upset than when I'd gone in sixteen hours earlier, running behind the paramedics as they rushed Leon into the emergency room. I'd just found out that Leon and

Jerome had been having a six-year affair, and the blow to my ego was ten times worse and a hundred times more devastating than any situation I'd ever been through in the past. Even more shocking was the way that son of a bitch stood his ground as he professed his love for my husband—no, his name is Leon. I will never call him my husband again.

My head was hurting me so bad I couldn't see straight as I stalked around the front of the hospital. I tried to calm myself, but my nerves were so bad I could hardly breathe. This was a woman's worst fear—to find out her husband was sleeping with someone else, and the pain was only intensified by the fact that the other person was a man. I had no idea how I was supposed to feel, but there was one thing I'd made up my mind about right away: I refused to be jealous.

Not of him, I told myself. *Not of a man. Not of Jerome!*

In this situation, jealousy would just be a waste of my emotional energy. I'd been around Jerome long enough to know that when it came to men sleeping with men, we women didn't have a chance anyway. If it had been another woman, I could compete. I could try harder, pay him more attention, make myself more attractive than the other woman, fuck him into submission. But with a man, there was just one simple fact: I had the wrong equipment. What good would it do me to be jealous of Jerome? If that's what Leon wanted, there was not a damn thing I would have been able to do to change it. Unless I found a way to grow a penis, and even if I could, I had no interest in doing that.

Now, don't get me wrong; I was angry. No, I was pissed the fuck off! But I wasn't going to be jealous. As sexy as Leon was, the fantasy was over. If he got up and walked out of that hospital bed right this minute, he would never get any of this ever again. Just the thought of sleeping with a man who slept with other men was just flat out disgusting if you ask me. I didn't even want to imagine what freakish acts they'd committed behind my back. Ugh!

I walked over to the curb and vomited. I retched and I retched until my stomach emptied the little bit of food that was in it.

"Miss, are you okay?"

I snapped out of my fog and glanced in the direction of the voice. It was one of the hospital security guards. I'm sure I looked like a hot mess standing there with tears running down my face, walking around in a daze. To top it off, I was standing in the drop-off area to the hospital and didn't even realize it.

"Yes, I'm okay. Thanks." I stepped back onto the curb.

"You sure?" He handed me a tissue and I wiped my face.

"I just got some really bad news."

"I'm sorry to hear that."

"So am I." I reached into my bag and took out a stick of gum. Without another word, I popped the gum in my mouth and walked away from the guard.

I wandered toward the parking lot, trying to figure out my next move. It took me a minute to realize I wasn't going to find my car. I had traveled to the hospital in the ambulance with Leon, and now I was stuck. I thought about calling Egypt to come pick me up, but I really didn't want to see her right now. Oh, she'd be sympathetic and everything, but she was happily married, and as bitter as I was feeling, I couldn't stand to be around her at the moment. I cared about Egypt, but inside I was hating, big-time. Why couldn't it have been her man who'd been fucking Jerome?

With no other options, I started walking west toward the Marriott hotel, which I planned on making my new home. I re-fused to go home, not to that house, not the house I shared with him, at least not until I figured out my next move.

As I walked down Marshall Street toward the hotel, I passed the Richmond Police Station. It was kind of an eerie feeling to know that Michael was behind those walls. If I was honest with myself, I had to accept some of the blame for what he'd done. I should have left him alone after the first time we broke it off, but I was torn between two lovers. I wanted both men, and I never really gave much thought to how unfair that was to Michael. I knew how he felt about me, so the way I rejected him must have been devastating to him. I might as well have put the gun in his hand and pulled the trigger.

Just that thought gave me pause. Suddenly, I wanted to go in-side and make sure he was okay. I stood on the sidewalk, looking up at the building for a minute, trying to decide if I was really going in. Then I came to my senses. Walking in there wasn't going to help Michael, and it damn sure wasn't going to help me. I could just imagine the headlines: LOVE TRIANGLE! WIFE VISITS HUSBAND'S SHOOTER IN PRISON. No, if I was going to help Michael, what I needed to do was get him a good lawyer and do it anonymously.

I turned to continue my journey to the Marriott, but I'd gone only a few steps before I heard Michael's voice calling out my name. He was coming down the precinct stairs.

"Michael . . . ," I said, and then I wasn't sure what else to say. After all, what does someone say to her ex-lover-turned-violent-offender? Then it finally dawned on me that in spite of his arrest, he was outside the prison walls, and now I was very confused. "I . . . you . . . What are you doing here? They told me they arrested you."

"They did. They just let me go." He sounded very happy, and he reached out to hug me, but I stepped back, looking at him warily.

"I didn't do it, Loraine," he explained. "I'm innocent. They've dropped the charges against me. I wasn't anywhere near your house yesterday."

I gasped. Was it possible that he was telling the truth? So many questions entered my mind at once, but I didn't even know where to start. "Please don't be lying to me, Michael. I couldn't take it if you were lying to me."

"I'm not, Loraine. Do you really think they would have let me out if I did it?"

I stared at him and tried to process what he was saying. Yes, he was out of jail, but I still didn't understand what was going on. Who else hated Leon enough to shoot him? When the officer told me they'd arrested Michael, they seemed pretty sure that they had the right man. But then again, after what just happened at the hospital with Leon and Jerome, I realized that no one could really be sure of anything, could they?

"I didn't shoot Leon," Michael said when he realized I was too stunned to say anything. He reached for me again, and this time I allowed him to wrap his arms around me. I collapsed against him and broke down in tears. Michael held me in his strong arms, and for that short period of time, I felt safe and loved.

"Michael, I'm sorry. This is all my fault."

"Shh . . . You don't have to apologize to me." He squeezed me tighter. "I love you, Loraine. All I want to do is take care of you."

"Do you mean that? Do you really mean that? Because right now, all I want is to be taken care of by a man who loves me."

"I've always meant it. I've loved you since I was fourteen. I don't know how to stop loving you."

I took hold of his hand. "Then take me home, Michael. Take me home and I swear we'll never look back. I just don't want to have to set foot in that house again."

"You mean that? What about Leon?" he asked skeptically.

"He's not the man I thought he was. You don't have to worry about him. He's the past; you're the future."

Michael leaned back and looked deeply into my eyes. "Baby, you don't ever have to go to that house again. My house is your house." He reached down and took my hand. "Come on. Let's go home."

Epilogue

31

It was a damp, overcast night, and I closed my coat to protect myself against the wind as I stood alone on the pedestrian walkway of Robert E. Lee Memorial Bridge. Looking down at the James River, I couldn't see much, but I could hear the fast-moving water smashing up against the rocks below. This bridge had become something of a lover's lane over the years, but I could also see why it was the location of choice for more suicides than any other bridge in the region.

Over the years, I'd met many brothers here to watch the sunset. As a matter of fact, this was the spot where Big Poppa and I first kissed, so I found it fitting to come here now that he'd passed away two days ago. Don't worry; I wasn't going to commit suicide. I just had so many things on my mind that I needed to clear up. So many demons that I had to put to rest before I could move on with my life.

I knew that Michael had been arrested for the shooting, but ever since Peter called me from Big Poppa's phone, I knew the truth. There was no doubt in my mind who had shot the man I loved. I just wanted to hear Peter admit it.

"Hey there, Lover Boy," I heard Peter say as he approached the spot where I was standing on the bridge. I felt a shudder pass through me. At another point in my life, I would have been so happy to have this gorgeous man calling me that. Now all I could think about was how much my "lover boy" behavior had cost me. Ron was gone, Loraine hated me, and Big Poppa had finally succumbed to his bullet wounds. And all because this one crazy fuck just couldn't let go of his fantasy that we were meant to be together. If only I could go back in time and change the way I'd handled my life. But there was no way to alter the past. All I could do now was get Peter to confess, and hopefully get justice for the people he'd hurt.

"Hello, Jerome," he said, leaning against the four-foot-high concrete railing. "I didn't think you were going to show up."

"I've been here almost twenty minutes. You're the one who's late."

He kind of chuckled to himself. "I know how long you've been here. I've been watching."

"Of course you were watching. I should have known." I struggled to contain my rage. I wanted to reach out and strangle him, but I had to accomplish what I was here to do: I had to get him to confess. "Why the hell is everything a game with you?"

He shook his head. "A game? On the contrary, my friend. Things are very serious, wouldn't you say? I mean, you have to understand things from my point of view. I may love you, but I damn sure don't trust you. I was halfway expecting there to be half a dozen undercover cops out here."

"Nope, just me. But if you thought this was some kind of a setup, why the hell did you come here in the first place?"

"Oh, I don't know . . . ," he said with an exaggerated sigh. "Call me a silly romantic, but I was sorta hoping you wanted to tell me you had finally come to your senses and we could be together. You did pick a romantic meeting spot, after all, despite the rain."

"I'm not here for romance."

"That's too bad. So, what did you want, Lover Boy?"

"I just need to know why."

"Whatever are you talking about?" I knew that the fake look of confusion on his face was meant to taunt me. He was getting under my skin and he was enjoying it.

"You know exactly what I'm talking about. There's only one way you could have gotten Big Poppa's phone." I was on the verge of tears when I asked, "Why did you have to shoot him? He didn't do anything to you!"

Peter continued to play with me. I swear he was stifling a giggle when he said, "What phone? Really, Jerome, what are you talking about? Have you been drinking? I didn't shoot anyone."

"Stop fucking playing games," I said, moving in closer. I had to stuff my hands in my pockets to keep from swinging at him.

He dropped the act and came back at me with just as much anger. "No, you stop. Stop fucking wasting my time," he said. "Open up your coat."

"What?"

"You asked me here for something, and it sure wasn't so that we could fuck. I'm gonna walk away right now if you don't prove that you're not wearing a wire."

"You think I'm wearing a wire?" I asked.

"I've been an investigative reporter for fifteen years, Jerome. I know all the cops' tricks."

I put my arms over my head. "Frisk me, then. You're not gonna find a wire. I got nothing to hide."

Peter hesitated for a second, like he was surprised his instinct was wrong this time. He looked a little confused when he checked me and discovered I wasn't recording our conversation.

"Hmph," he said, trying to play it cool. "It wouldn't matter anyway. You really think I'd be stupid enough to leave behind any evidence that could connect me to that shooting? C'mon now. You know I'm too good to slip up like that. Not a fingerprint to be found, and that cell phone is long gone. . . . I mean, I'm good, and on top of that, they really made it easy for me."

"They?"

"Yeah, *they.* I told you I would go after every one of your lovers until you were mine. I was prepared to take them out one by one if I had to. That kid Ron wasn't even a challenge. Shoot, he was so unstable to begin with. I knew that he'd go off the deep end if I put those pictures in the paper."

I felt sick as an image of Ron's lifeless body came into my mind.

"Now, your beloved Big Poppa, of course, was more of a challenge. It took me forever to find out who he was. You know giving him a gate key and a garage opener so he could hide his car when he visited was pretty smart. But once Ron died and you disappeared, he must have been pretty flustered. He started getting careless. I mean really . . . having takeout food delivered to your house when you weren't even in town? Not smart, especially when I had the pizza-delivery guy on my payroll. And then he was stupid enough to park in front of your house. I may not have been able to drive my car in, but I walked right past those toy cops while they were sleeping all the time while you were away." He shook his head. "It took all of ten minutes for my contact with police to track down his license plate number."

Peter was becoming more animated as he spoke, like he was enjoying the storytelling, proud of his ability to track down my lovers and destroy them—and me.

"You know I didn't even realize he was your friend Loraine's husband until I showed up at their house." He shook his index finger at me. "You know, you're really not a nice person, Jerome. I mean, you can say whatever you want about me, but that's some pretty low shit, fucking your best friend's husband."

"It wasn't something I planned to happen. But sometimes we do things we wouldn't necessarily do for love."

He nodded his understanding. "You know, I was thinking the same thing as I shot Big Poppa's ass."

Tears were rolling down my face at this point. "Why?" was all I could manage to say.

He rolled his eyes and spoke to me like an impatient parent scolding his child. "How many times do I have to tell you? If I can't have you, then no one will. No one takes what belongs to me!"

"What the fuck are you talking about? No one took anything from you. They didn't deserve to be hurt."

"They took you from me, Jerome. Don't you understand? We're supposed to be together. They were getting in the way of you being with me!"

"You're crazy. We will never be together."

He leaned back casually against the railing. "Oh, I wouldn't be too sure about that. Sooner or later, you'll understand that there is no one else for you. The next man you try to get with, I'll kill him too. I'll kill them all if they get between us."

So this was Peter's plan for the rest of my life: stalk me forever and destroy anyone I get close to, until I came back to him. It was time to put an end to this insanity.

"Then you leave me no choice. I guess I'll have to take matters into my own hands." I took a step toward him.

"You and what army?" He easily pushed me off with a derisive laugh. "You can't stop me. You never could—that's why your precious little Ron and Big Poppa are dead now."

I stomped my foot and screamed, "I've heard enough, Peter!"

My outburst took Peter momentarily by surprise, but it had the desired effect. I looked up at the man who had heard my signal and was quickly advancing on Peter from behind.

Peter turned to look in the direction of my gaze just in time to see the man reach out for him. He grabbed Peter by the collar and lifted him into the air. I moved quickly to his side and seized Peter's feet.

"You remember Freddie, don't you, Peter? You thought it was pretty funny when his wife was chasing him around Outback, didn't you?"

"Wait!" Peter yelled, sounding on the verge of tears. "Jerome, I'm sorry. I won't bother you anymore. Please don't do this! I can't swim!"

"Oh, it's not the water you have to worry about; it's the rocks," Freddie mocked as Peter went over the side. "Bon voyage, motherfucker."

We heard Peter's screams all the way down. Then, silence. It was over.

"Man, I almost didn't think you were going to give me the signal," Freddie said.

"Yeah, you know, for a second I thought about backing out, trying to convince him to turn himself in. But in the end, it never would have worked. That crazy motherfucker would have been chasing me for the rest of my life."

Freddie shook his head. "Damn shame." He looked over the edge, down into the darkness. "You think he's dead?"

"If the rocks didn't get him, the rapids will." I stepped away from the railing. I was ready to go home. "Did you take care of all the loose ends?" I asked as Freddie and I started walking.

"Yeah. This guy didn't even have any firewalls protecting his computer."

When I met Freddie and learned he was a computer whiz, I never could have imagined that I'd be asking him to put his skills to use in this way. I guess we never really know where life will lead us, do we?

"Half an hour ago," Freddie explained, "everyone on his Facebook page got an update that he was sick of life and didn't want to live anymore."

I drew in a deep, refreshing breath of night air. "Thanks, man."

"No problem, Jerome. That son of a bitch deserved it. We still on for Thursday afternoon?"

"Freddie, I hope you don't mind, but I'm going to need a little time before I can go down that road again."

"Hey, after all you've been through, I totally understand."

Dear Readers,

Wow! I hope you enjoyed reading *Big Girls Do Cry* and *Torn Between Two Lovers* as much as I enjoyed writing them. I have to admit I'm a little tired now. For you folks that say I don't write them fast enough, well, I want you to know that putting out two books in one year is not an easy task, but I do hope to put out two books next year also.

So, I hope you'll look out for my new church drama, *The Choir Director*, in late January or early February 2011, where we meet smooth-talking Anthony Mackie and the women who love him. Then, later in the year, look out for something new and a bit edgier, with the first installment of *The Family Business*, a trilogy like none you've ever read. Who are the Dumpsons, and why does everyone fear them?

Well, that's it for me. Again, I hope you enjoyed my latest works. If you get a chance, hit me up on urbanbooks@hotmail.com, or visit my web site at www.carlweber.net. Until then, be safe, and leave the drama to me.

Peace,

Carl Weber

TORN BETWEEN TWO LOVERS

CARL WEBER

ABOUT THIS GUIDE

The following questions are designed to facilitate discussion in and among reading groups.

1. Did you think Leon was involved with his therapist at first?

2. Was Loraine wrong for taking Leon to the same spa she and Michael visited?

3. Would you have told your spouse if you found out that you were sexually molested as a child?

4. At any time did you think Michael was losing it?

5. Were you happy when Jerome and Ron hooked back up? Or did you think Jerome should have left him alone?

6. What were your thoughts when Michael first purchased the gun? Was there ever a time you thought he'd used it?

7. Was Loraine wrong for breaking up Michael's relationship with Celeste?

8. Have you ever had a stalker?

9. Did you know who Big Poppa was? Were you surprised at all?

10. Who do you think Big Poppa really loved?

11. What would you do if you found out that your dying spouse was unfaithful?

12. What was your opinion of Peter? Did he get what he deserved?

13. On a scale of one to ten, what did you think of this book?

14. Which character or characters would you like to see again?

15. What is your favorite Carl Weber book?

The Big Girls Book Series

Something on the Side
Big Girls Do Cry

From *Something on the Side*

1

Tammy

I love my life.

I love my life. I love my marriage. I love my husband. I love my kids. I love my BMW, and I love my house. Oh, did I say I love my life? Well, if I didn't, I love my life. I really love my life.

I stepped out of my BMW X3, then opened the back driver-side door and picked up four trays of food lying on a towel on the backseat. I had only about twenty minutes before the girls would be over for our book club meeting, but I'd already dropped off my two kids, Michael and Lisa, at the sitter, so they weren't going to be a problem. Now all I had to do was to arrange the food and get my husband out of the house. The food was easy, thanks to Poor Freddy's Rib Shack over on Linden Boulevard in South Jamaica. I merely had to remove the tops of the trays from the ribs, collard greens, candied yams, and macaroni and cheese, pull out a couple bottles of wine from the fridge, and voilà, dinner is served. My husband was another thing entirely. He was going to need my personal attention before he left the house.

I entered my house and placed the food on the island in the kitchen, then looked around the room with admiration. We'd been living in our Jamaica Estates home for more than a year now, and I still couldn't believe how beautiful it was. My kitchen had black granite countertops, stainless-steel appliances, and handcrafted cherrywood cabinets. It looked like something out of a home-remodeling magazine, and so did the rest of our house. By the way, did I say I love my life? God, do I love my life and the man who provides it for me.

Speaking of the man who provides for me, I headed down the hall to the room we called our den. This room was my husband's sanctuary—mainly because of the fifty-two-inch plasma television hanging on the wall and the nine hundred and some odd channels DIRECTV provided. I walked into the den, and there he was, the love of my life, my husband, Tim. By most women's standards, Tim wasn't all that on the outside. He was short and skinny, only five-eight, one hundred and forty pounds, with a dark brown complexion. Don't get me wrong—my husband wasn't a bad-looking man at all. He just wasn't the type of man who would stop a sister dead in her tracks when he walked by. To truly see Tim's beauty, you have to look within him, because his beauty was his intellect, his courteousness, and his uncanny ability to make people feel good about themselves. Tim was just a very special man, with a magnetic personality, and it only took a few minutes in his presence for everyone who'd ever met him to see it.

Tim smiled as he stood up to greet me. "Hey, sexy," he whispered, staring at me as if I were a celebrity and he were a starstruck fan. "Damn, baby, your hair looks great."

I blushed, swaying my head from side to side to show off my new three-hundred-fifty-dollar weave. I walked farther into the room. When I was close enough, Tim wrapped his thin arms around my full-figured waist. Our lips met, and he squeezed me tightly. A warm feeling flooded my body as his tongue entered my mouth. Just like the first time we'd ever kissed, my body felt like it was melting in his arms. I loved the way Tim kissed me. His kisses always made me feel wanted. When Tim kissed me, I felt like I was the sexiest woman on the planet.

When we broke our kiss, Tim glanced at his watch. "Baby, I could kiss you all night, but if I'm not mistaken, your book club meeting is getting ready to start, isn't it?"

I sighed to show my annoyance, then nodded my head. "Yeah, they'll be here in about ten, fifteen minutes."

"Well, I better get outta here, then. You girls don't need me around here getting in your hair. My virgin ears might overhear something they're not supposed to, and the next thing you know, I'll be traumatized for the rest of my life. You wouldn't want that on your conscience, would you?" He chuckled.

"Hell no, not if you put it that way. 'Cause, honey, I am not going to raise two kids by myself, so you need to make yourself a plate and get the heck outta here." He laughed at me, then kissed me gently on the lips.

"Aw-ight, you don't have to get indignant. I'm going," he teased.

"Where're you headed anyway?" I asked. A smart wife always knew where her man was.

"Well, I was thinking about going down to Benny's Bar to watch the game, but my boy Willie Martin called and said they were looking for a fourth person to play spades over at his house, so I decided to head over there. You know how I love playing Spades," Tim said with a big grin. "Besides, like I said before, I know you girls need your privacy."

Tim was considerate like that. Whenever we'd have our girls' night, he'd always go bowling or go to a bar with his friends until I'd call him to let him know that our little gathering was over. He always took my feelings into account and gave me space. I loved him for that, especially after hearing so many horror stories from my friends about the jealous way other men acted.

Tim was a good man, probably a better man than I deserved, which is why I loved him more than I loved myself. And believe it or not, that was a tall order for a smart and sexy egomaniac like myself. But at the same time, my momma didn't raise no fool. Although I loved and even trusted Tim, I didn't love or trust his whorish friends or those hoochies who hung around the bars and bowling alleys he frequented. So, before I let him leave the house, I always made sure I took care of my business in one way or another. And that was just what I was about to do when I reached for his fly—take care of my business.

"What're you doing?" He glanced at my hand but showed no sign of protest. "Your friends are gonna be here any minute, you know."

"Well, my friends are gonna have to wait. I got something to do," I said matter-of-factly. "Besides, this ain't gonna take but a minute. Momma got skills . . . or have you forgotten since last night?"

He shrugged his shoulders and said with a smirk, "Hey, I'm from Missouri, the Show Me State, so I don't remember shit. You got to show me, baby."

I cocked my head to the right, looking up at him. "Is that right? You don't remember shit, huh? Well, don't worry, 'cause I'm about to show you, and trust me, this time you're not going to forget a damn thing." I pulled down his pants and then his boxers. Out sprang Momma's love handle. Mmm, mmm, mmm, I've got to say, for a short, skinny man, my husband sure was packing. I looked down at it, then smiled. "Mmm, chocolate. I love chocolate." And on that note, I fell to my knees, let my bag slide off my shoulder, and got to work trying to find out how many licks it took to get to the center of my husband's Tootsie Pop.

About five minutes later, my mission was accomplished. I'd revived my husband's memory of exactly who I was and what I could do. Tim was grinning from ear to ear as he pulled up his pants—and not a minute too soon, because just as I reached for my bag to reapply my lipstick, the doorbell rang. The first thought that came to my mind was that it was probably my mother. She was always on time, while the other members of my book club were usually fashionably late. I don't know who came up with the phrase "CP time," but whoever it was sure knew what the hell they were talking about. You couldn't get six black people to all show up on time if you were handing out hundred-dollar bills.

Tim finished buckling his pants, then went up front to answer the door. I finished reapplying my makeup, then followed him. Just as I suspected, it was my mother ringing the bell. My mother wasn't an official member of our book club, but she never missed a meeting or a chance to take home a week's worth of leftovers for my brother and stepdad after the meeting was over. Truth is, the only reason she wasn't an official member of our book club was because she was too cheap to pay the twenty-dollar-a-month dues for the food and wine we served at each meeting. I loved my mom, but she was one cheap-ass woman.

My mother hadn't even gotten comfortable on the sofa when, surprisingly, the doorbell rang again. Once again, Tim answered the door while I fixed four plates of food for him and his card-playing friends. Walking through the door were the Conner sisters—my best friend Egypt and her older sister Isis. Egypt and I had been best friends since the third grade. She was probably the only woman I trusted in the world. That's why sometime before she left, I needed to ask her a very personal favor, probably the biggest favor I'd ever asked anyone.

Egypt and Isis were followed five minutes later by the two ladies I considered to be the life of any book club meeting, my very spirited and passionate Delta Sigma Theta line sister Nikki and her crazy-ass roommate, Tiny. My husband let them in on his way out to his spades game. As soon as the door was closed and Tim was out of sight, Tiny started yelling, "BGBC in the house," then cupped her ear, waiting for our reply.

We didn't disappoint her, as a chorus of "BGBC in the house!" was shouted back at her. BGBC were the initials of our book club and stood for *Big Girls Book Club*. We had one rule and one rule only: If you're not at least a size 14, you can't be a member. You could be an honorary member, but not a member. It wasn't personal; it was just something we big girls needed to do for us. Anyway, we'd never really had to exclude anyone from our club. I didn't know too many sisters over thirty-five who were under a size 14. And the ones who I did know were usually so stuck-up I wouldn't have wanted them in my house anyway.

About fifteen minutes later, my cousin and our final member, hot-to-trot Coco Brown, showed up wearing an all-white, form-fitting outfit I wouldn't have been caught dead in. I know I sound like I'm hatin', but that's only because I am. I couldn't stand the tight shit Coco wore. And the thing I hated the most about her outfits was that she actually looked cute in them. Coco was a big girl just like the rest of us, but her overly attractive face and curvy figure made her look like Toccara, the plus-size model from that show *America's Next Top Model*. Not that I looked bad. Hell, you couldn't tell me I wasn't cute. And I could dress my ass off too. It's just that the way I carried my weight made me look more like my girl MóNique from *The Parkers*. I was a more sophisticated big girl.

Taking all that into account, some of my dislike for Coco had nothing to do with her clothes or her looks. It had to do with the fact that she was a whore. That's right, I said it. She was a whore—an admitted ho, at that. Coco had been screwing brothers for money and gifts since we were teenagers. And to make matters worse, she especially liked to mess around with married men. Oh, and trust me, she didn't really care whose husband she messed with as long as she got what she wanted. Now, if it was up to me, she wouldn't even be in the book club, but the girls all seemed to like her phony behind, and she met our size requirement, so I was SOL on that. I will say this, though: If I ever catch that woman trying to put the moves on my husband, cousin or not, she is gonna have some problems. And the first problem she was gonna have was getting my size 14 shoe out of the crack of her fat ass.

As soon as Coco entered the room, she seemed to be trying to take over the meeting before it even got started. She was stirring everybody up, talking about the book and asking a whole bunch of questions before I could even start the meeting. And when she and Isis started talking about the sex scenes in the book, I put an abrupt end to their conversation.

"Hold up. Y'all know we don't start no meeting this way." I wasn't yelling, but I had definitely raised my voice. "Coco, you need to sit your tail down so we can start this meeting properly."

Coco rolled her eyes at me and frowned, waving her hand at Nikki, who had already made herself a plate, asking her to slide over. Once Nikki moved, Coco sat down. Now all eyes were on me like they should be. I was the book club president, and this was my show, not Coco's—or anybody else's, for that matter. But she still had something to say.

"Please, Tammy, you should've got this meeting started the minute I walked in the door, because this book was off the damn chain." Coco high-fived Nikki.

"I know the book was good, Coco. I chose it, didn't I?" I know I probably sounded a little arrogant, but I couldn't help it. Ever since we were kids, Coco was always trying to take over shit and get all the attention. "Well, once again, here we are. Before I ask my momma to open the meeting with a prayer, I just hope everyone enjoyed this month's selection as much as my husband and I did."

Egypt raised her eyebrows, then said, "Wait a minute. Tim read this book?"

"No, but he got a lot of pleasure out of the fact that I did. Can you say chapter twenty-three?" I had to turn away from them I was blushing so bad.

"You go, girl," Isis said with a laugh. "I ain't mad at you."

"Let me find out you an undercover freak," Coco added.

"What can I tell you? The story did things to me. It was an extremely erotic read." Everybody was smiling and nodding their heads.

"It's about to be a helluva lot more erotic in here if you get to the point and start the meeting," Coco interjected, then turned to my mom. "I don't mean no disrespect, Mrs. Turner, but we're about to get our sex talk on."

"Well, then let's bow our heads, 'cause this prayer is about the only Christian thing we're going to talk about tonight. Forget chapter twenty-three. Can you say chapters four and seven?" my mother said devilishly, right before she bowed her head to begin our prayer. From that point on, I knew it was gonna be one hell of a meeting, and Tim would appreciate it later when he came home and found me more than ready for round number two.

From *Big Girls Do Cry*

Prologue

The taxi pulled into the circular driveway, rolling to a stop in front of the expensive double oak doors of the large brick colonial. Roscoe, the driver, a fortysomething dark-skinned man, placed the car in park and turned toward the woman in the back seat.

He smiled to himself. He liked the way she looked. She was just his type of woman, thick and pretty, with skin like a chocolate bar. Oh, and even more enticing were her large, melon-sized breasts. Yes, sir, Roscoe sure loved a woman with big titties and some meat on her bones. And this one was as fine as she could be. He had thought about asking for her number or perhaps offering to show her around Richmond when she first entered his cab at the airport. Over the years, Roscoe had bedded many a lonely female passenger after picking them up at Richmond's bus station or airport. All it usually took was some small talk and an invitation to one of the city's many bars or eateries for a drink. But this sister had spent most of the ride on her cell phone, probably comforting some insecure boyfriend or husband afraid her fine ass would wind up with a Southern charmer like him. Now that they had reached her final destination, he would have to make his move quick if he was going to bed this plus-sized beauty.

"That'll be forty dollars, ma'am." He smiled, revealing a mouth full of gold teeth.

Tammy, a woman in her late thirties, didn't notice his unattractive smile or his country accent, things that would have surely caught her attention and gotten under her skin if she weren't already preoccupied with looking at the house they'd just pulled in front of. She would never admit it to anyone back home, but a twinge of jealousy swept through her body as she stared at the house. The large colonial was at least twice the size of her Jamaica Estates home back in New York, and compared to her yard, this house's land appeared to be big enough to hold a football field or two.

This has to be the wrong address, she told herself. *They can't afford this.*

"Are you sure we're at the right house?" she asked without moving her head, her mind still trying to process what she saw before her.

"Yes, ma'am. You said Four James River Lane, didn't you?"

Tammy glanced at the paper in her hand, then looked at the large number 4 on the house. "Yes, that's what I said."

But this can't be her house. It just can't be. Tammy's thoughts were consumed by jealousy.

"Then this is where you want to be. Do you want some help with your bags?"

She reached in her purse for her wallet. "How much do I owe you?"

"Forty dollars. I usually charge fifty when I come out here to Chesterfield County, but havin' a pretty woman such as yourself in my cab, I feel like I owe you. Maybe I could show you around town. They're having an all-you-can-eat rib festival down at

Shockoe Bottom tonight. My name's Roscoe." He offered her his hand.

Tammy rolled her eyes and shook her head, flashing the two-carat diamond ring on her finger.

"My name is *Married*," she snapped, "and my husband's name is Foot in Your Ass."

She was about to go on putting this homely, gold-tooth fool in his place, but before she could continue, she saw someone come out of the house. A light-skinned woman, big, but not quite as large as Tammy, came running toward the taxi. That's when Tammy knew there was definitely no mistake; she was at the right address. But how the hell did her best friend get a Mc-Mansion like this? And who the hell were they robbing to pay for it?

Tammy handed the driver two twenty-dollar bills, then stepped out of the car. She was usually a pretty good tipper, but with that country-ass come-on the driver just tried, she figured he'd forfeited his tip.

Egypt threw her arms around Tammy's neck and pulled her in closely. "Tammy, girl, I missed you something awful." She placed a huge red-lipstick kiss on Tammy's cheek.

Tammy smiled at Egypt when she let her go. She'd missed her friend too. They had a lot of catching up to do, and even more importantly, she wanted to know how Egypt and her new husband, Rashad, could afford such a nice house when they earned far less than she and her husband did. Or did they?

"Girl, you moving on up, aren't you?"

"You think? Come on in and let me show you around." Egypt was grinning from ear to ear. She knew Tammy had to be envious, and she loved every minute of it. "You can leave her bags by the front door," Egypt instructed Roscoe.

Tammy followed her friend. Yes, she wanted to see her house. She wanted to see if the inside looked anything like the outside.

Tammy and Egypt had known each other for almost thirty years and had been best friends since they'd met. But even best friends could have rivalries. As close as they were, the two of them had played a one-upsmanship game when it came to material things since they were teenagers. Tammy, however, had been winning this competition handily the past ten years because of her marriage to her successful husband, Tim. She had thought the title would be hers for a lifetime, but as she walked into the flawlessly decorated foyer of Egypt's house for the first time, she was afraid that the tides had changed.

As a matter of fact, she was so amazed as she followed her friend from room to room that she barely noticed the people sitting in the large family room until Egypt shouted out, "BGBC in the house!" and the people in the room all stood in unison and echoed, "BGBC in the house!"

Tammy couldn't help but blush. She smiled at Egypt, who gave her a thumbs-up. It was one of those moments in a woman's life when she feels a sense of accomplishment. One of Tammy's dreams was actually becoming a reality, and she couldn't have been prouder. She'd come to Richmond for two reasons. One of them was to catch up with her friend, who she hadn't seen since her wedding the year before. The other was to be in attendance at the first meeting of the Richmond chapter of the Big Girls Book Club. She'd started the club five years ago in New York with only one rule: you had to be at least a size 16 to become a member. With the success of that first book club, which had swelled from five members to almost thirty, Tammy had the dream that someday there would be BGBC groups in cities all over the country. Her best friend was helping her realize that dream.

Tammy glanced around the room. There were more than a dozen people there, but she felt as if she knew four of them personally because of her conversations with Egypt. Of course, there was Isis, Egypt's older sister and former member of the New York chapter of the BGBC. She'd moved down to Richmond a few months ago to get away from the hustle and bustle of New York, or so she said. Only time would tell if that was her true motivation. Tammy had a suspicion that there were more personal reasons involving her sister.

Then there was Loraine Farrow, Egypt's boss and one of Richmond's leading businesswomen. Loraine was a tall, well-dressed woman in her early forties. Despite her 275-pound figure, she was very attractive. She owned a large public-relations firm in town. Tammy liked her right off the bat, not just because

Egypt had said she was a take-charge woman who didn't take smack from anyone, but also because of the way Loraine carried herself. It was obvious from one glance that she was a woman of class who deserved respect.

While Loraine exuded everything good about being a black woman in her forties, the woman standing next to her represented everything bad. She had a very attractive face, with two huge dimples on both cheeks, but Tammy's first impression of LaQueta Brown was that she was a hot mess. Her clothes were too loud; her blouse was way too tight for a woman her size; her skirt was too short; and from what Egypt had told her, she was so damn boisterous it could make you sick. She put the *g* in *ghetto* and really didn't care.

But as much as Tammy was appalled by having LaQueta in the BGBC, there was only one member she disapproved of on principle. That member was Jerome. Oh, yes, Jerome was a man, a very handsome man at that. Perhaps even a little too handsome. Tammy argued with Egypt about him for almost two weeks on the phone, but her friend wouldn't budge on including him in her BGBC chapter.

"Our club has only one rule, Tammy," Egypt had argued, "and that's that members have to be at least a size sixteen. Well, we put him in a dress, and he meets the size requirements."

"But he's a man, Egypt!"

"So? It's not against the rules. And he reads everything from romance novels to Mary Monroe to L. A. Banks."

Tammy was so puzzled by Egypt's insistence on Jerome joining that she accused her of sleeping with him. "Sounds to me like someone's trying to keep their boyfriend close and not raise any eyebrows."

Of course, she got a denial and some very choice words back.

"You know what? Fuck you, Tammy. I've never cheated on my husband. Not once! Can you say the same?"

There was silence; then Tammy said, "That was cold, girl."

Egypt didn't mean to be so spiteful and throw Tammy's business in her face, but sometimes it was the only way to keep her friend in line. "I'm sorry, but you need to stop. You know I would never mess around on Rashad."

"I also never thought you'd invite a man into our book club. So, as the president, I must say no."

"You may be the president, but this is my chapter, and if I can't run it the way I see fit, then there isn't going to be a Richmond chapter."

Egypt knew how much Tammy wanted the club to go national. She took a gamble, but the gamble paid off. Tammy finally gave in, and the core for the Richmond chapter was formed.

Now, Tammy settled in to a plush armchair in Egypt's living room and watched as her friend got the meeting under way

---

Prologue

It was Father's Day at First Jamaica Ministries, the largest church in Queens, New York, and the pews were filled to capacity with those honoring the men in their lives. Bishop T. K. Wilson, the pastor of the church, was in top form as he pranced around the pulpit, preaching on what it truly means to be a father and a man in this upside-down world of ours. His sermon was so powerful and his words so inspiring that he brought grown men to tears and had some of the more animated women jumping out of their seats and fainting in the aisles. He touched on the responsibilities of being a husband and a father. What made his sermon so special was that he tied it all into the word of God so well that even the children had no problem understanding it.

When he finished his sermon, everyone in the building felt enlightened, but the celebration was far from over because when the bishop sat down, the choir stood up and the collection plate went around. Halfway through the first song, everyone in the church was on their feet, singing, clapping, and paying tithes.

"Hallelujah!" the bishop said as the choir finished their third selection and sat down. "Wasn't that wonderful? Praise God! Thank you, Jesus. There is nothing like having a good song with the Word. Can the church say amen?"

"Amen!" the congregation shouted back in unison.

"Now, as most of you know from my sermon, today is Father's Day, the day we're supposed to honor our fathers and husbands." He held on to the microphone as he paced from one end of the pulpit to the other. "I know some of you are ready to go home and barbecue with Dad, maybe go to the beach with him, maybe even just sit in front of the TV and watch the game with him, but before you leave, there is one order of business that we have to take care of."

Bishop Wilson returned to the center of the pulpit and placed the microphone back in its holder, then reached under the podium and removed a large plaque. "You see, every year on Father's Day, we give out a Man of the Year Award and a scholarship in the recipient's name. This year, though, I think the committee's outdone themselves with their choice of Man of the Year, and in my opinion, this year's award is way overdue. Not just because I consider the recipient a personal friend, and not just because he's an outstanding father and husband, but also because of all the hours he's spent on making your choir one of the best in the entire country."

As the bishop turned to the choir, the entire congregation rose to their feet in anticipation of his announcement. "Now, ladies and gentlemen, brothers and sisters, it is my absolute honor to announce that the winner of the First Jamaica Ministries Man of the Year Award is our choir director, Mr. Jackie Robinson Moss!"

The crowd erupted in cheers and applause when Jackie, a tall, handsome, olive-skinned man with green eyes, stepped from in front of the choir and approached the pulpit, where the bishop awaited him with the plaque.

Bishop Wilson shook Jackie's hand, then gave him the award. He was about to relinquish the podium to the Man of the Year when he heard a woman shout, "Bishop! Bishop! I'd like to say a few words, if you don't mind."

The bishop smiled his approval when he saw the woman. "Sure. We'd be glad to hear a few words from you, Deaconess Moss. I mean, after all, who knows Jackie better than his wife?"

There was another round of applause as she got up from her seat in the deacon's row and slowly made her way to the pulpit. She was a good-looking, brown-skinned woman in her mid-forties and had been married to Jackie, her college sweetheart, for almost twenty years. Approaching the pulpit, she shook the bishop's hand before stepping up to the podium and adjusting the microphone.

"Hello. As you know, my name is Deaconess Eleanor Moss, and you've bestowed the honor of Man of the Year on my husband." She turned to give Jackie a look of contempt, then turned back to the crowd to deliver totally unexpected words. "I'm sorry to say it, but you have made a grave mistake in giving him this award. Unfortunately, my husband is not the man you think he is. And he is definitely not the man I thought he was. Not anywhere close to it."

Members of the congregation started squirming in their seats. Some were reacting to the uncomfortable awkwardness of the situation, while others were eagerly anticipating some juicy drama getting ready to take place.

Realizing that things weren't going exactly as planned, Bishop Wilson turned to Jackie and mouthed, "What is she talking about?"

Jackie shrugged his shoulders, looking dumbfounded. It was obvious he was as clueless as everyone else about his wife's strange behavior. The two men stood by helplessly as she continued the speech that would destroy all the good feelings Bishop Wilson had created with his Father's Day sermon.

"I know this is going to be hard for many of you to believe, but trust me, it was even harder for me. I've been married to this man for twenty years." She took a breath and straightened her back, as if what she was about to say required all of her strength. Then she delivered the final blow. "But I think you should all know my husband is a homosexual."

It was as if her words sucked all the air out of the room. The entire church went silent, except for one woman who shouted, "Shut up!" sarcastically.

At this time, Eleanor's two best friends, Lisa Mae and Kathy, began handing out quarter-inch–thick xeroxed pamphlets down each row, beginning in the back of the church.

"If you look at the pamphlets the sisters are handing out," Eleanor continued, "you will see copies of my husband's journal, which I found hidden in the ceiling panels of our basement, along with some pretty filthy Polaroids. I'm sorry I could not furnish originals, but I need them for my divorce. The highlighted entries show affairs Jackie has had with different male members of our choir and congregation. You will see names, dates, times, personal comments in some cases, and even preferred activities. I know some of you will be upset by this, but I honestly believe it's better to know now rather than later. I myself am about to get an AIDS test."

Her business complete, she turned around, walked up to her husband, and slapped him across the face as hard as she could before she walked out of the church.

The congregants, who had now all received copies of the pamphlet, were furiously paging through them. As the sound of rustling pages and confused whispers filled the sanctuary, Bishop Wilson stood, slack-jawed, staring at the man who had been his choir director for seven years. He'd heard rumors over the years about Jackie but he figured those spreading the gossip were just jealous and catering to the stereotype of a gay choir director. Never once did he think the rumors might actually be accurate.

Now he had to ask the question: "My God, man, is this true?"

Jackie didn't answer. He simply turned toward the door by the side of the pulpit. Bishop Wilson followed his gaze and watched four male choir members sneaking out of their seats, headed toward an exit. Two of them were active members of the church, proud family men. If someone had told the bishop that these men were involved in homosexual affairs, he would have placed wagers against it; yet, here they were, their escape practically an admission of guilt.

An abrupt scream startled him, and he turned to the pews to see a physical altercation erupt between a deacon and his wife. He ran to break things up, wondering just how much chaos this incident had introduced into his church.

The Bishop

1

I stepped off the elevator and onto the third-floor oncology unit of Columbia Presbyterian Hospital, holding the hand of my wife, Monique. We were accompanied by my good friend of more than twenty years, Deacon Maxwell Frye. As we walked down the hall, I recognized the pungent odor of medical disinfectant. It didn't matter what hospital I visited; the smell was always the same, and it seemed to embed itself in my nostrils. I hated it because it always reminded me of the imminent deaths of the people in the rooms around me. Oh, I'd learned to tolerate it over the years, especially since visiting people in their last days was part of being the pastor of First Jamaica Ministries, but today's visit wasn't just to any old parishioner on his deathbed. No, today's visit was much closer to home and way more personal for me and Deacon Frye. We were here to see our very dear friend James Black, who was dying of lung cancer.

"T. K., Monique, get your behinds in here," James coughed out when he saw us standing in the entrance to his room. He hadn't seen Deacon Frye yet. Despite his condition, it was obvious he was glad to see us.

As we entered the room, Monique's grip tightened around my hand. I could tell she was struggling to conceal her shock at just how bad James looked. I had tried to prepare my wife before we arrived, but words couldn't describe how much he had deteriorated.

This was the first time Monique had seen him since he'd pled guilty to murder charges a little over a year ago. I still couldn't believe he'd willingly gone to jail for a crime he didn't commit, but I guess some parents will go to any lengths to protect their children. Can't say whether I would have done the same, but I was glad I had never been put into that position. He'd been given a twenty-year sentence, but I pulled some strings after a recent visit when I heard his prognosis, and he was released for medical reasons. Cancer had taken a vibrant, six-foot-tall, two-hundred-pound man and turned him into a talking skeleton. Even more unbelievable was the fact that his hair was completely white. He seemed to have aged twenty years in less than a year's time.

It didn't take my wife long to gather her composure. In a matter of seconds, she leaned in and wrapped her arms around James to give him a kiss on the cheek. She shot me a pointed look when she spotted a picture of his two grown children sitting on the night table beside his bed. Monique hated the idea that his daughter and son were both missing in action and hadn't come to see their father once since his arrest. I didn't fault her for feeling that way, but I knew a little more about the situation than she did. I'd made a promise to James not to share what I knew, even with her.

"James, I've got a surprise visitor for you." I gestured toward the door and watched as a grin broke out across James's face.

"Wait, don't tell me, T. K. You finally pulled it off. You got Holly Robinson-Peete to divorce her husband and become my personal nurse until the Lord takes me home."

"Holly Robinson? Have you lost your mind? Here you are supposedly on your deathbed and the woman you want to spend your last days with is Holly Robinson-Peete? You couldn't set the bar any higher than that? I mean, come on, James. If you're going to fantasize about a woman, you need to go all out and do it with a bang!" Maxwell joked as he appeared in the doorway. He and James had always been like that.

"Well, I'll be damned. Maxwell Frye, how the hell are you?"

James smiled from ear to ear. "I'll be honest, brother. I didn't think I'd see you again in this lifetime. How long you back for?"

Deacon Frye had been in Iraq for almost five years. His company, Maxwell Enterprises, was a minority contractor for the government and was doing infrastructure work in Iraq. One of the stipulations in the contract was that he oversee things personally. He'd been back stateside only a few times briefly since.

Maxwell walked around to the far side of James's bed and gave him a hug. "I'm back for good. I was having some heart problems, and they had to fix me up with a pacemaker. Sorry I'm just getting around to seeing you, but I'm only now starting to get readjusted. Things have really changed around here." He glanced over at me and my wife. We had not been married when Maxwell left for Iraq. Like many other church members, Maxwell was surprised by my decision to marry Monique.

"Change . . . don't I know it," James said. "It's good to see you, Maxwell. The Wilsons over there are gonna need your help keeping these church folks in line."

"Well, you know I'll do whatever I can, James."

"I know you will. I feel better about things already."

James turned to my wife as Maxwell took a seat in the chair on the other side of his bed. "So, Monique, how are you? You're looking good as ever." He looked at me and winked. "No offense, old friend, but your wife just gets finer and you just keep getting older."

"I know that's right," Maxwell added.

"None taken." I chuckled. "I think she looks pretty good myself. That's why I married her, remember? And as far as getting old, well, I'm like a bottle of wine: I get better with time."

"Mmph, you sure do, honey." Monique gave me a smile, then turned her attention back to James. "To answer your question, I'm doing fine. What about you? How you doing? You look good."

James laughed. "Girl, I swear, you have fit right into that first lady's role, haven't you?"

I watched my beautiful wife blush.

James spoke gently to her. "Now, I know I look like crap, so you don't have to lie to me, Mo." He sighed. "I know my best days are behind me. I made my peace with that a long time ago. I'm ready to die."

"Who said anything about you dying? You're probably going to outlive us all, you old coot." I was trying to break up the mood in a way only a true friend could do.

"If I do live that long, it's only to be a pain in your ass, T. K." he joked, forcing himself to sit up. My wife helped him by propping a pillow behind his neck. "But seriously, I'm tired and I'm ready to go home. I just hope the Lord's willing to let me in the door."

I hated to hear him say things like that, so I tried to offer him some encouragement. "I don't think you have to worry about that, James. I think you've sacrificed enough, don't you? The Lord—"

James shot me a glance that basically said, "Let's not go there."

I nodded my head out of respect for his condition and his feelings, but that didn't mean I had to like it. That man had sacrificed his entire life for the love of his family, and he had been willing to die in a jail cell because of it.

James quickly changed the subject. "So, Mo, how about him? He taking care of you the way he's supposed to?"

She reached out to take my hand as she answered. "I couldn't have asked for a better man. I couldn't have asked for a better life."

"That's what I like to hear." James nodded his approval. "Are those wenches in the church treating you all right? They're not trying to run over you, are they? 'Cause all you have to do is kick one of them in the ass and the rest will fall right in line," he said with a laugh.

"Oh, you don't have to worry about that. I've got them right where I want them." Monique and I had had a rocky start to our relationship, because certain members of the church—mostly female—thought her rumored past was too dicey for her to be considered a candidate for the role of first lady after my first wife died. She was strong, though, and had withstood the storm. Now she was well respected and loved by most church members.

Even those who had been adamantly against our marriage knew enough to treat her cordially now and kept their opinions to themselves.

"Besides," she continued, "we have bigger problems than that at the church. With—" She stopped when I squeezed her hand, signaling for her to shut up, but it was too late. James's body might have been failing him, but his mind was still sharp as ever.

He sat up straight as a board, ignoring the pain. There were three things James loved most in this world: his two children and our church. He knew the ins and outs of church politics like nobody's business. He'd been both a deacon and a member of the board of trustees just as long as I'd been pastor, and we made quite a formidable team. But now, with him being sick, I didn't have the heart to tell him that what we had built together over the years was slowly crumbling.

"What's going on at the church, T. K.?" He was staring directly at me, and his eyes did not budge from my face.

"It's nothing, James, seriously. I can handle it." I glanced over at my wife, who was trying to apologize with her eyes. I loved her to death, but just this once I wished she had kept her big mouth shut.

When I turned back to James, he was still staring at me, waiting for an answer.

"What, do I look stupid? If it was nothing, you would have told me by now. Now spill it. I wanna know what's going on at my church."

My church. He was still claiming ownership in our church, even though most of our members had turned their backs on him when he was arrested for murder. If they only knew how selfless he really was.

He looked at Maxwell. "What do you know about this, Deacon Frye?"

"I've been trying to—"

I cut off Maxwell before he could put himself in a bad position. "He knows what I told him and nothing more."

"So tell me what you know, T. K.," James demanded.

I began to pace back and forth in front of his bed. "James, you've got other things to worry about. You don't need this nonsense. You need to concentrate on your health."

"Dammit, T. K., my health ain't worth a damn right now. Face it—I'm dying. The only thing I got left is that church. Now, are you going to tell me what's going on, or do I have to make some calls and find out myself?"

"Tell him, honey," Monique prodded. "You two have always worked well together. Maybe he can come up with an idea to help."

"Thank you, Mo," James said matter-of-factly.

I continued pacing for a short while before I finally sat down next to my wife and looked at my friend, ready to tell him the truth. "The church is in trouble financially. We're down about thirty-five percent in attendance and almost forty-two percent in revenue. The board's thinking about closing down the school next year if things don't get better, and that's just the beginning."

"What?" His body tensed up angrily. "I built that school. We had plenty of money put aside in the school fund before I went to prison."

"Priorities changed when you were arrested. The country went into recession. People aren't giving as much as they used to. The rates on our adjustable mortgages have reset much higher than anyone expected. I tried to keep things simple, but Simone Wilcox was voted chairwoman of the board of trustees, and last year she pushed to have money directed to the building of new senior housing. We've got a lot of working capital tied up in that project."

I could see James running the numbers through his head. He'd always been good with figures, which was why he'd been elected chairman of the board of trustees despite his reputation as a womanizer.

"You gotta be kidding me. We can't afford to be building at a time like this. What's that heifer Wilcox trying to do, bankrupt the church? Why the hell you let them elect that woman head of my board, I don't know. She's not her father, T. K. Simone Wilcox ain't out for anyone but herself. The woman's a diva with an agenda. Trust me, she's always got something up her sleeve."

"You of all people would know, James," Maxwell joked, taking a jab at the fact that James used to sleep with Simone.

"Don't get smart, Maxwell. That was a long time ago."

"Not to her," my wife commented. "But in her defense, James, she's got an MBA, and she runs one of the largest car dealerships in the area."

"Oh, give me a break. That's only because her daddy retired and didn't have any sons to leave it to. She could never have built a dealership like Wilcox Motors by herself. I bet you half her staff has already left. I'm surprised it's still standing." James shook his head. "I know she's your friend, Mo, but Simone's best asset is between her legs. I could tell you some stories."

"That's chauvinistic, James. You're just hating on her because she's a successful woman," Monique snapped.

"No, that's just realistic. There are plenty of women who could have done a good job as chairwoman. Simone's just not one of them."

"Like who?"

I glanced over at Maxwell, shaking my head. My wife had just opened up a can of worms she might not be able to close.

"Did you guys take Lisa Mae into consideration?"

Monique scrunched her face like there was a bad odor in the room at the mention of Lisa Mae, a one-time rival for my affection. "No, we did not consider *that woman*," Monique told him. She didn't know I knew it, but she'd secretly campaigned to make sure Lisa Mae never had a shot at the chairmanship. "However, Simone couldn't have been but so incompetent. Things were going pretty well until attendance dropped."

James was clearly frustrated by this news. "Answer me this: Why'd attendance drop? Something must have pissed everybody off. What, did Simone start charging a fee at the door for people to get in? People don't just stop going to church en masse."

"They do when the choir director's trying to sleep with their husbands and sons." Monique was trying to hold back a laugh. The situation definitely wasn't funny, but just like plenty of other people, my wife had a weakness for gossip.

James looked at me with a frown. "Oh Lord, it was Jackie, wasn't it?"

I nodded.

"Well, I guess he wasn't as harmless as you thought. I told you we needed to get rid of that SOB years ago, T. K."

Clearly, James had been much better than I at judging the truth. I'd wanted to dismiss it as rumors. James had always predicted Jackie would cause trouble, and he had been painfully correct.

"Yeah, you did." There was nothing I hated more than listening to one of James's I-told-you-so rants. "I just wish I had listened to you. That man's wife has got the whole congregation in an uproar."

"What's she doing?"

"She found his journal. Turns out all those rumors were true, and he recorded every sordid detail in that diary," I admitted. "She didn't waste any time spreading the news either. Over a third of the men in the choir found themselves in that journal in some capacity or another, and the other two-thirds were considered guilty by association."

I felt badly for Jackie's wife, and part of me could understand why she reacted the way she did. You can imagine how devastating the discovery must have been for her, and, well, misery does love company. Unfortunately, her coping method left me with a huge problem on my hands. Word spread quickly, and within two weeks, the entire choir disbanded, even though Jackie had already been fired and was no longer attending the church. My wife and I had been trying to put it back together to no avail. I never knew how hard a choir director's job was until then.

"Now we've got no choir," I said as I finished summing up the turmoil we'd been struggling with. "Now, I'm a heck of a preacher if I do say so myself, James, but nothing goes better with the Word than music. Our choir has always been a cornerstone of our church. Putting my ego aside, wasn't it you who once told me that half the people in the pews on Sunday were there to hear the choir and not me?"

He chuckled. "Yeah, I guess I did say that, didn't I?"

"Well, from where I'm sitting, you're sounding more and more like a prophet."

"Man, I can't believe something like this could take down the church," Maxwell added.

"Neither can I. Plus, when you add that to the financial troubles we're having, it's like the perfect storm. To be honest, I don't know what we're gonna do. We've got a huge balloon payment on one of the church's mortgages next year."

"You're right. Only thing that's gonna save us is getting people back in the church. What about Savannah Dickens? Maybe we can get her to help," he suggested. At one time, Savannah Dickens's voice could light a fire in the soul of even the greatest heathen. But like so many other things, that had changed too. She left the church to start a career singing pop music. It looked like she was going to make it, too, until she got hooked on drugs. She fell hard and she fell fast, and no one in the church had seen or heard from her since.

"Already thought of that, James, but it looks like Sister Savannah has lost her way to drugs. She's not even a member of our church anymore."

"I know what we have to do, honey," Monique interrupted. "We have to hire a choir director. But not just any old choir director. We need someone young, someone so talented and so charismatic that he can put together a choir that will blow the roof off the church. This choir has to be so good that everyone in the borough of Queens will be fighting for a good seat in the pews just to hear them sing."

"I understand what you're saying, baby, but do you have anyone in mind? 'Cause I don't know anybody like that."

James snapped his fingers. "I do!" His sunken features suddenly looked a little brighter. "T. K., do you remember last year before I got locked up when we went to visit Reverend Simmons's church in Jarratt, Virginia?"

"Mmm-hmm. What about it?"

"Do you remember his choir? There was only about ten of them, but they were some kind of good."

"Yeah," I said with excitement. "I remember. They had that

young kid leading them with all the Kirk Franklin moves and the BeBe Winans voice. What was his name?"

We sat quietly for a moment, both of us trying to remember. James finally recalled it. "Aaron," he announced with a smile. "His name was Aaron Mackie. And he's exactly what we need." He folded his arms. "He's the total package, T. K. He's got looks, charisma, and sex appeal in a church kind of way. There's no doubt in my mind the boy could save our church."

"Well, then, I guess I'm gonna have to go down to Virginia and have a talk with Mr. Aaron Mackie."